COWBOY
STORIES

GRIT, HORSES, AND FAITH

MIKE ROBERTSON

Charlie & Suzy
Cook —
I am very pleased to
see you interested in a
book of mine — But truly
hope you will enjoy it.
and keep reading —
Mike Robertson
Nov 21- 2015.

Cowboy Stories: Grit, Horses, and Faith

Published by Wheatmark®
1760 East River Road, Suite 145
Tucson, Arizona 85718 U.S.A.
www.wheatmark.com

ISBN: 978-1-62787-057-3
LCCN: 2013949312

*"Trust in the Lord with all your heart and
lean not on your own understanding;
in all your ways acknowledge him, and
he will make your paths straight."*

Proverbs 3:5-6

*"And we know that in all things God works
for the good of those who love him, who
have been called according to his purpose"*

Romans 8:28

*"God gives his best to those that
leave the choice to Him"*

Mike Robertson

CONTENTS

FOREWORD

"THE OLD BROWN"

by Marcia Hoffman; First appearing in
Western Horseman Magazine, @ 1948 and as
memorized by Mike Robertson when he was a boy

> *The air was so blue*
> *You could cut it in two,*
> *And the beat of the auctioneer's cry*
> *Fairly deadened your sense,*

To the course of events
And the price of the horseflesh ran high,

There was bidding that day
That broke records, they say,
Til' nobody dared blink an eye;
Then a brown was led in
To the hypnotic din,
But it seemed no one wanted to buy.

He was fourteen or so
But he'd had a rough go,
He'd been short on good feed, as a rule;
And the auctioneer knew
That he must push him through,
Or the heat of the buying would cool.

The auctioneer did
Get only one bid,
He said, "Sold!" and the horse left the lot;
And five kids were delighted
And wildly excited
When they saw what their Daddy had bought.

Without reservation
They showed their elation,
They brushed him and combed him down sleek;
They fed him more hay
In that one single day
Than the old horse had seen in a week.

FOREWORD

He had more darned attention,
Well-meant intervention-
Much more than he needed, by rights!
He had plenty of grain
And a roof when it rained,
And a blanket to wear on cold nights.

In no time at all
He would come to a call,
And he added some sass to his gait,
He got foxy and fat
And snorty, at that,
While he carried his tail out straight.

Now when he's not eating
He's patiently treating
The kids to a ride high in style;
Through Indian fights
And childhood delights,
Mile after mile after mile.

Well, value is strange,
It can waiver and change,
And it happened precisely that way;
At the time that they got him
A few dollars bought him
And no price could buy him today.

This is the poem that Mike Robertson recited to me, the first time I sat down with him to talk about these stories. He had memorized the poem as a boy, after having seen it in a magazine and has carried it in his heart ever since. It speaks a lot about him and his character, that this poem touched him at such an early age and that he still finds it important enough that he continues to share it whenever he can, some 70 years later.

Mike is from a period of time in our American history that is quickly disappearing and he embodies all the good qualities humans can have, that are by today's standards considered "old fashioned" and sadly rare.

I first met Mike after a Cowboy church service, which is held in his auction barn every Sunday for the small congregation of folks that live out near him. I was staying with some dear friends, one of whom happens to be the Pastor of said Cowboy church, so I tagged along one Sunday.

The first thing you notice when you meet him, is that you become mesmerized by him. He has rough hewn hands that decades of hard work have created, and sun-drenched lines on his face from smiles, and miles, and decades spent in the elements. He looks like he stepped right out of a Hollywood casting company in response to a request for an old American cowboy! He has an easy smile and a twinkle in his eye and his gait deceptively covers a lot of ground, so the first time I followed him out to the mare and foal pasture to see the babies, he had to wait so I could catch up. He was too much of a gentleman to ever have brought that up, but I noticed.

At almost 80 years old, he still works with horses and cattle every day, and still has a quarter horse breeding operation that consistently turns out well put together, mentally solid and kind horses, ready to work. He is also still an auctioneer and the first Saturday of every month, you can find him in action at their facility, helping out neighbors far and wide to sell their horses for the best price possible.

Mike has been writing things down his entire life, whenever he wasn't on a horse. It has been my pleasure to help him put his collection of stories about people and animals he has known, wrapped in lessons of character, integrity, and Faith. He told me that his hope was to write something that perhaps someone else might like to read someday. I think he has accomplished that in spades.

Sara Dent

INTRODUCTION

Iwas born to extremely good Irish parents in a little place called Two Dot, Montana, in 1936. At 20 years of age I bought a little ranch from three old bachelors from that area, and with my brother and the rest of my family we ran that ranch for 25 years.

In the early 1980s I moved to Benson, Arizona, where I have lived for the past 30 or more years. I have spent the past 30 years ranching and building a sale and auction business where we continue to have monthly horse auctions the second Saturday of every month. We also have an American Quarter Horse breeding program, under the Keyhole brand.

I have always been an avid reader, reading almost exclusively about History, Cowboys, Ranching, and a occasionally a few biographies of famous people. I have also always had the urge to write.

Most of my life I have stayed quite busy, ranching, working with horses, and working horse auctions. I kept thinking someday as I got older, or if got crippled up, or some other such set back, I would have the time and would like to tell some stories about the things I have seen and experienced along the way.

Being blessed to not have been crippled or have anything else happen, I find myself older and in a position to be able to share my stories. The only restraints I put on myself in telling stories was that they all have to be true.

INTRODUCTION

A few of the stories I tell were told to me long ago, so I suppose they now have some contribution of my opinion and my take on the story that was told to me. The stories I have shared here that I did not write, happened before my time. Just like my own stories however, they all have some point, lesson, or example which might offer a little food for thought to someone new reading it.

I have lived a lot of my life being alone and at times quite a way out into the hills and out of contact with other people. When I did spend time with people, I gathered valuable material to write about. This time spent ranching and away from other people may not have provided me with anything in line with the vocabulary or writing skill that good authors possess, but my stories are all authentic. My stories are all hands on personal perspectives and opinions I have come to through my life experiences.

The stories I have written come from my experiences ranching and working cattle and horses. I have ranched with many solid character type people who shared with me their upstanding values and helped shape who I am today. Once in awhile I came across a person or two who did not share those same good values. The memorable experiences I have had with all the people I have come across have contributed to my stories.

Living a life ranching, a person becomes very close to his neighbors and must rely on his fellow man. A person also feels connected to animals both wild and domestic, as well as the earth and all of nature. Most important of all, a person relies daily on God who created it all and guides us. I very much believe that it is God who inspires me with the words that I use to tell my stories, and guides the message and lessons shared in each story. I would feel very rewarded and pleased if someone who read one of my stories felt in any way entertained or inspired.

Life in general has been very good to me, and while I am not wealthy money wise, I have been extremely wealthy in the blessings of good health, great friends of every description, and a wonderful family. I am also blessed to have the support of God and the good people from my church, without whom this book would not be possible.

OLD FRENCHY

I often think about an old story I was told many years ago, which took place before my time, so it is based strictly on hearsay. But I always thought it contained a pretty good lesson and, often throughout the years, I see similar examples to remind me of the truths it represents.

It all took place back a little while after the Indians were relocated onto reservations and had reconciled the fact that this was going to be their new way of life.

1

I believe the man in this story was pretty typical of most of those older men who finally settled for the reservation life. Everyone called him Frenchy, and I never heard how he had obtained his name but a tremendous number of people got to know him and held him in extremely high regard.

As Frenchy got older and his life started to be winding down it seemed he withdrew from his family more and more and reverted back into not only his past days but very much into the past days of his ancestors and tribal customs and ways. His main event each day was to take care of a few cattle he owned and his favorite horses. He would then find a warm spot out of sight at the edge of a clearing and out of the wind on cold winter days or a nice cool shady spot of much the same description on hot summer days and dream of past times he longed to relive and relate back to buffalo hunts, battles, powwows, summer and winter treks, and all of the past that was no longer available to him.

As he would sit and dream about and relive these days, he would carve small statues of all the animals, which used to mean so much to his people.

His little ranch, which he lived on and had made his living from for some years, kind of dwindled away to falling down corrals and barns, a few small odds and ends of old wagons, or occasionally a trailer or an old plow rusting away here and there half buried in the dust and weeds, only slight reminders of once part of his past. But these things did not bother him and went totally unnoticed by him.

Carvings of his little bears, a doe and her fawn, an

occasional buffalo or a wolf or mountain lion were completely detailed and life-like. They were everywhere and
new ones carved and created daily were a testament to his
daily labors.

Eventually, people from everywhere started coming
by to see some of his carvings and to listen to his stories
about the things he new of each animal he carved. People
generally would ask him what he would take for one of
his carvings. He would usually answer them with his
Indian accent, "You lak him? Take him." He would hardly
pay any attention to whether they took them or not. But
unbeknownst to anyone, it seemed to make him feel good
inside to think someone else would like to have one of his
carvings.

Often times when people who had heard tales of the
carvings, or who had known someone who possessed one,
would stop by Frenchy's home, but upon arriving would
then wonder why they had bothered to come by because
of the appearance of the place. But upon meeting Frenchy
and seeing his work, people would feel a strange close-
ness and connection to him, and then when they touched a
carving of a bear or an antelope, some claimed they could
actually smell the breath or feel the heart beating of the
carved animal. Once that happened, a deep desire to own
some would come over them, and people would offer
Frenchy a lot of money to secure a carving to take home.
No matter what they offered, Frenchy would tell them that
was plenty, and would usually throw in a second carving
for free. Frenchy did not carve these figurines in order to
make a profit. Frenchy made these figurines out of love
and appreciation for the animals they represented, and

money would never compare to the value of that. The true reward that Frenchy received from the people that came to meet him and see his carvings, was realizing that others could appreciate that the animals and his carvings meant to him culturally and emotionally, and that people seemed to understand that Frenchy loved the carvings for what they represented, and not for any sort of monetary wealth he could collect simply for creating them. Many people came to meet Frenchy and spend time with him, while at the same time purchasing carvings before they left. Most of these folks spent a few hours with Frenchy, getting to know him a bit, and these people always left feeling like they had just spent time with a rare and special person. Frenchy continued to feel like he was meant to continue carving more animals.

Frenchy had raised a boy and a girl who he was very proud of, although his son grew up to bring him some grief. The son was a pretty good rodeo cowboy whose rodeo accomplishments were some of Frenchy's most enjoyable and proud memories, but his other actions like drinking, doing some petty robberies, and fighting, had ended up in numerous trips to jail for the son. And then there was the incidents of the son taking some of Frenchy's carvings. After a few years of watching people come by to meet his Father and seeing them leave with his carvings, the son realized he could make a considerable amount of money by selling them himself. The son would occasionally pick some up and take them with him when he went out on the road to travel, and provide him with a nice amount of spending money, a case or two of beer, and maybe even a bottle or two of whiskey. Frenchy never knew how many the son had taken, and had been disposed of is such a disgraceful manner. Frenchy resolved himself to the idea that his son would no doubt one-day hit the big time in the rodeo, but I don't know if that ever happened.

On the other hand and in contrast to the son, Frenchy's daughter had gone to school and had become quite successful. By most everyone's standards, she was very pretty as well as smart, and she landed a job with a local bank off of the reservation. She was a hard worker, and earned a number of promotions. The daughter was considered a real asset to everyone as a loan officer and bank official by Indian and white people alike. As her success grew she became acquainted with a large number of people who learned of her father's carvings and she was responsible for encouraging many people from near and far away to stop by to see his work and meet her Father.

While all of this was going on, Frenchy's wife was beginning to develop a huge self-conscious attitude about their life style, the fact that their home looked very old and rundown and they didn't even have any indoor plumbing. Their water was brought into the house in a bucket from the spring and there was no bathroom at all-only an outhouse. Along with these things, Frenchy's father, Grandpier, who was about 100 years old, lived on their property in a badly patched and worn old teepee and he dressed as nearly as he could exactly like his ancestors from his childhood days. Just as Frenchy spent his days carving animals and reliving the past, his wife was trying desperately to clean up the property, rebuild and remodel their home, and trying every way she could to hide Grandpier and have him removed.

The wife was highly embarrassed that people with means would drive in daily to look at Frenchy's carvings and see their home and way of life that she saw as so primitive. She would complain to Frenchy how he should be working on the place and that no one who came truly appreciated his stories and his carvings. She felt that they were just amazed at their wasted place, which he took for granted and would do nothing about. She would tell Frenchy that she felt like she had to pray daily that no one who stopped there ever got a look at Grandpier. She was very annoyed by the state of their homestead and it was the cause of many disagreements between she and Frenchy. After a number of years of these disagreements, Frenchy's daughter bought a house in town for her mother. Frenchy's wife then moved off their little ranch and became happily lost in the larger population of the town, seemingly at ease and enjoying all the modern conveniences a more "civilized" life style had to offer, even though she enjoyed it all alone.

After awhile Frenchy got too old and his sight and his hands could no longer carve his beloved animals and the reminders of a happier time in his life. The accuracy of the detail in his carvings began to look blurry, through Frenchy's eyes, as well as to others. Frenchy could not tolerate the thought of his beloved carvings being blurry, and so he put away his carving tools. The realization that he would no longer be bringing home a beautiful tree limb or block of wood that he could magically make animals appear from. Frenchy slowly surrendered his thoughts to the realization that his favorite pastime, his purpose in life was slowly disappearing, just as his perfect way of life as a young man had disappeared. Frenchy recognized that his ability to carve his magical animals disappearing was parallel to many of the actual animals disappearing also, as "civilization" grew, and the old ways became more and more blurred into the past.

People in the local area eventually forgot about Frenchy and ceased to come by the house. The carvings became legend, relics of the past, and Frenchy quietly passed away a very old man, with many memories of a time and way of life gone by.

You could never say Frenchy was a famous man, but in a few shiny, tall modern office buildings, every so often, a man in a fancy suit will gently pick up a wood carving of an animal, and wonder about the man who had created it, and the magical life that contributed to its existence. The legacy of Frenchy lives on, and those stories that he shared with the people who were lucky enough to have one of his carvings enable him to be forever loved, respected, and remembered for all the magic he had created and the traditions he had unknowingly preserved.

THE GOOD LITTLE
PAIR OF OUTLAWS

Old Roddy had sure been around a long time and had been a horse and mule man his entire life. As a young man, he had learned to ride pretty good, broke a lot of colts, and made most of his living as a cowboy. Often, he made a few extra dollars hiring out as a rough string rider for some of the ranchers.

At some point in his life, he learned that he could make a little more money with his teams and a fresno or other implements. He broadened his horse business to breaking and hiring out teams. For the biggest share of his life, his income was derived from horses in some form or another.

But also along the way, he began to see that industry was starting to depend more and more on heavy equipment and gas burning tractors. He started noticing a little less call for his business with his teams. To make up his losses, he decided to restore and rebuild wagons, buggies, collectable horse drawn farm implements. He also worked at trading horses and teams to people who had a use for them.

During this process, he began to realize that many years had passed and he was getting older. Along with this fact, his health started slipping and he found himself doctoring a few serious ailments like high blood pressure, severe arthritis, and diabetes. He also knew he had become excessively overweight, and that his eyesight had almost left him. Like lots of people, he understood that he could no longer do most of the things he had enjoyed doing his whole life. Realizing he was starting into his eighties, he began backing down and not doing too much of anything. But his yard was still cluttered with wagon and buggy parts; good ones, used ones, pieces, and relics. All of these were just kind of left sitting around because the demand had slowly dwindled away and his ability to fix them up, or make any kind of use out of them, had just ceased to happen. This happened so gradually, he hardly realized it was going on. Finally, it got down to just a whole lot of old rotting has-beens sitting all around his yard, and Roddy didn't notice them any more. He really couldn't even see them most of the time. The same was true of harnesses, collars, and hames stock piled and laying everywhere— twisted, tangled, torn up, and scattered in endless piles.

His old corrals and buildings got run down and started leaning and they constituted a pretty serious eye sore to most of his neighbors, but Roddy just didn't notice hardly any of it. He memorized his way around through little trails to get where he wanted to go so it just seemed okay to him. His biggest worry about it all was that he didn't feel good, he couldn't see anymore, and he seemed to be getting to the end of his rope. His old legs had become very unstable under his excessive weight. He would often fall exactly like a power pole. If he tripped a little, or got bumped by his dog or a horse, there was no stopping him; he just crashed to the ground, falling on things that hurt his knees, ribs, and skinned his face and hands. He felt like he had become pretty useless and he wasn't liking it very much.

But there was one thing he could still do, and he did it religiously, every single day. He had bought a little team of mules for about $900 apiece. Every morning that little pair of mules needed to be fed, watered, and groomed and that was Roddy's entire purpose for waking up in the morning. It had become such a routine for him that he just took it for granted that probably everyone on earth had to get up in the morning, feed, and take care of their horses or mules. It never occurred to him that he might not have that job to do as long as he still woke up each day. In his eyes, if he lived one more day, he still needed his team. After he had got them all taken care of, he loved more than anything to harness them, hook them up to his one remaining little spring wagon, and drive them down to the Café for coffee with his old friends. It's what made his day, and what made his friends' day to look out the window and see that he had made it one more time.

They would see him driving down the street in his buggy and watch as the little brown mules would pull up to exactly the same spot in front of the Café every morning. Stopping on their own in front of just the right power pole where old Roddy, taking as much as thirty minutes, would dawdle down off the seat, hobble up by those two little fellers, and tie them to the pole. Eventually, he'd make his way inside the Café to be greeted with all kinds of friendly jokes and accusations by his old friends and then sit and discuss the gossip and events of the morning. This was surely the routine day after day. And it went on for quite a while.

Each morning, as Roddy would start home it was also the same routine. He'd untie the mules and turn them out into the street. They would faithfully stand and wait for him to hobble around to the front of his wagon where he would stumble and bump into their hips and tail ends. He'd hang on to the harness, and while they both stood very still, never moving a muscle, Roddy would climb up into the seat, gather up his lines, bark out a command to them, and they would start the wagon with a slight lurch and slowly drive him home where the whole thing happened again, day in and day out. Whatever Roddy was unable to see, those little mules took into account and handled it very well. They most certainly did all the looking on the trip both ways. Old Roddy and his friends use to laugh and conclude these mules had more sense than most of the other drivers on the street that early in the morning. For a few years, they took the best of care of Roddy and saw to it he got to the Café and back home safely. It seemed to be good for them and sure was the one thing that kept Roddy going.

Everyone expected to hear any day that something had happened to Roddy and no one would have ever been surprised at all to hear of some accident or that he had failed to wake up, but on this chilly winter morning, Roddy pulled up as usual in front of the Café and went inside. At the usual hour, he came back out and, going step by step through the exact ritual, started the routine of climbing up onto the wagon seat. The little mules, as chilly as it was outside, were faithfully standing as still as a pair of boulders. Because it was cold this morning, Roddy had put a blanket on the seat, and as he reached for the seat to pull himself up onto the wagon, he accidentally got a hold of his blanket instead of the seat. When he pulled himself up, the blanket slid and caused him to fall over backwards, down between the two little mules. Everyone who saw the accident said the little mules did not so much as flick a tail, even though they knew something pretty bad had just happened—they did not move a muscle. Roddy fell over backwards and landed hard onto the wagon tongue. Because of his age, and the state of his health; he broke his neck and was dead.

Many bystanders helped to get Roddy out from between the mules and they all marveled at the way the mules stood still, although they were scared. Immediately, the story broke that old Roddy's mules had finally run off and killed him.

The local newspaper flashed the headlines: *Elderly man killed by run away mules*. The farther away the story got, the more gruesome it became, even at one point claiming that the mules ran into a train. No possibility was left out. The mules instantly became known as the pair of mules that killed the old man. Eventually, Roddy's widow decided she had better sell them. But no one wanted any part of them, as they had really made a reputation. She finally decided to send them into the horse auction about a hundred miles away.

She hired one of Roddy's closest old friends to load them up and haul them to the sale. By this time, without Roddy's daily brushing, feeding, and caring for them, the little mules came into the sale with long feet. Only the evidence of a shoe left on the foot of one of the mules let prospective buyers figure out that they'd ever been shod. They were very longhaired, had many burrs in their manes and tails, and looked badly neglected. They stood totally bewildered and each tried to hide behind the other one. All the people and the excitement at the horse sale worried them very much. And, of course, several people volunteered information saying that they were the run away pair of mules that killed that old guy here a year or two ago and nobody has ever hooked them up since."

Because they arrived late at the sale, they were hurried through without any one cleaning them up at all. Sell them and get rid of them for whatever they bring. They were caught and led into the sale ring looking very much like two little wild Bureau of Land Management Mustangs. Their little eyes were sore from the burrs and bugged out in fear. They were extremely scared and nervous at all of the noise and hustle of the sale. They were called the "little run away killer mules."

Sitting there in the crowd that day were some very good traders, cowboys, ranchers, and wannabes; all of them sat and stared at the little pair of mules that had entered the ring. But among the people in that crowd sat a little red headed guy, who was considered sort of a problem at the sale. He was usually a little bit inebriated, and was, in fact, that day,. He would often buy a horse and then couldn't pay for it. Sometimes he had bought horses, and then he and his wife would fight because she didn't want him to spend the money. Red, as he was known, would only show up once in awhile, but he happened to be there that day. His shirt tail was hanging out, and he had his cap cocked on the side of his head. Tobacco juice was running down both sides of his mouth, and he had been voicing a lot of opinions about people's horses, which no one paid much attention to, except that it did disrupt the sale a little.

The Auctioneer started trying to get a bid on the little mules—so much apiece and take both of them. Keep the pair together. Someone finally bid $100 a head and before the Auctioneer acknowledged the bid, little Red exploded from his seat and shouted, "Why that's ridiculous! I'll bet that is a dandy little pair of mules, just look at them. It sticks out all over them." He held up his hand spread out and said, "$500 each and I'll take them both." The Auctioneer was worried that Red would not back up his commitment, but he took the bid and prayed some one would take him off the hook. He tried hard to obtain even $10 a head more, but no one there could see the good in them. At last, the Auctioneer sold them to Red for $500 each. He was sure that Red had never in his life had a thousand dollars in his pocket at one time, ever.

But little Red was very happy. He jumped out of his seat, followed the little mules out of the ring, and back to their pen. He went immediately to currying burrs out of their manes and tails. He was definitely very happy. He went straight into the office and wrote a check for them. The check, for the first time, turned out good, and Red thought he had made the greatest find of his life. Even his wife agreed and was happy.

Whether Red was able to see through the mules and realize the good in them, or whether he just sat there and had an inspiration that day, no one got to ask him. He took the little mules home, went back to feeding them, and did, indeed, give them a good home. He got himself a fancy little four-seated buggy and started hiring out to people for weddings, birthday parties, and general buggy rides. He built up a pretty good reputation with his mule team and went into the biggest business he had ever known. He loved those little mules and turned down many chances to sell them. He kept them looking nice, drove them with care, and even had the foresight to buy them that day at the sale. As one old rancher put it, "One thing about it, when you see Red going down the road with those mules, it's further proof that those two little mules are still the smartest ones on the road."

GLEN
NEBBLE

Along in the spring of 1946, I was going to school in a two-room schoolhouse in Two Dot, Montana. I guess I was in about the fifth grade, as I was 10 years old.

World War II had ended and was creating a very exciting time that even I, at that age, could recognize. Our friends, neighbors, and relatives were returning back home from the war, except the ones who would not return.

Many of the very good old ranches in the area were still showing the results of the depression of 1929, the drought and dry years of most all of the 1920s, and the absence of many of the younger members of a lot of families who were sacrificed to participate in the huge world war, which America had been forced into for at least the first half of the 1940s.

It had begun to rain again and pastures and crops were beginning to grow and rivers were beginning to flow. Rationing had come to an end. People began to see some advance in prices, and ranches could once again begin to operate.

A man named Bill Fox had managed to purchase an old third generation ranch from out along Big Elk Creek about six miles south of Two Dot. He had bought about 20,000 acres of falling down buildings and fences, heavily covered fields and pastures of thistle and tumble weeds, and a good portion of a dry river bed, which, in normal times, was a very adequate stretch of a beautiful river stocked with fish, beaver, tall cottonwood trees, and willows; a real rancher's paradise.

The few remaining members of the third generation owners and occupiers of this ranch had gone onto other ventures, been killed in the war with Japan, yielded to old age retirement, or the other alternative. The main thing most people saw on the ranch, which for many years was a very productive and efficient producing concern, was now a most obvious example of total neglect. But Bill Fox was a true rancher and an optimistic believer that, with his hard work and effort, he would soon reproduce an efficient and thriving operation.

One of the people he brought in with him to operate this new enterprise was a tall, lanky, cowboy-type manager named Clyde Nebble. I remember meeting Clyde and his wife and their infant son. They worked for Bill and managed his ranch for the next couple of years and were well accepted and recognized as successful newcomers to the Twodot area.

I went to school four more years and then had to go about 12 miles farther down the road to Harlowton to high school. It was somewhere along this time period that Clyde all of a sudden passed away. It was a big surprise as he was young—at least no more than 40 years old. It was very difficult for everyone to understand, but by then things were getting busier, it was just accepted, and life went on.

For a while I was aware that Mrs. Nebble and her son moved into Two Dot and she went to work for the man who owned the only general store and post office in town. By that time the store, one bar, and a hotel were still operating. Time went on and a boy in high school who was interested in pursuing a career in ranching didn't have much interest or time to keep track of what other people were doing.

By the end of the next six years, I had finished high school and bought a little ranch about 25 miles north of Two Dot. While a lot of this was taking place, Two Dot had dwindled away a little more as the storekeeper had sold out all of his holdings in Two Dot and had married the widow Nebble and, with her son, who was now around 15 or 16 years old, moved to Harlowton. He operated a filling station for a while, then tried his hand at another business, and finally just settled for retirement.

The problem was that her son, whose name was Glen, was becoming a thorn in his stepfather's side. It seemed like his mother would side along with her new husband and Glen was beginning to figure out that he was a real problem to them both. This problem had been going on for enough years that it was leaving Glen very mixed up and unable to sort out just what it was that he was doing so wrong and could find no way to remedy the problem. He just knew that he was very frustrated, lonely, and lost. He was doing very poorly in school, became totally withdrawn, had no friends, and no one to guide him. He believed that he had no future and no hope to ever do anything constructive.

At last his parents decided Glen should be sent to the

reform school in Miles City, Montana, about 300 miles down on the east end of the state. There he could have access to a therapist who might figure out what was wrong with him. And so it was done.

I knew nothing about any of this and only learned about it from Glen later on when he himself told me the saddest story I have ever heard, as I will now explain.

Along in the early 1960s, the Soil Conservation Service in Montana came up with a program to replenish farm and ranch lands in Montana by seeding new grasses or reseeding old pastures, irrigation systems, and fencing projects. On the ranch I had bought, I qualified for some of this money to fence new pastures and improve grazing; I had put in for and was awarded about six miles of fencing. It had to be done in a certain amount of time and according to their specifications, but I went for it and was doing it.

One day a car drove into my ranch and a young boy, probably about 17 years old, walked up and asked me if I could give him a job. He was a very handsome boy and reminded me of a famous movie actor about that time called Steve McQueen. Other than that, I didn't know him at all. He finally told me he was Glen Nebble and had heard of me back when he was a little boy in Two Dot. I was extremely surprised and grateful to get to know him. I could see he was inexperienced and very self-conscious as he talked to me, but we made a deal. I was having a tough time trying to start up this ranch I had bought and to establish a cowherd, but I felt I could use some help on my new fencing job and, with the government paying most of the bill, I could pay him to build fence.

I let him move into an old sheep wagon I had on the

ranch and we started preparing to work—not knowing anything about Glen's troubled life. The last time I had seen him, he was a very cute little baby boy whom I thought had a good old cowboy for a dad.

As the work started to progress, I found that I had hired a young kid who knew he didn't know too much, but was ambitious and eager to learn. He also had a tremendous intent to please. He would get very embarrassed when he had to admit that he didn't know how to do something or if he caused any kind of extra effort or trouble, which almost never happened.

I was by this time barely starting into my early 30s and was married and starting a family. I did not consider myself as anybody's mentor nor did I have anything much to offer in the way of advice or experience, as I myself had already experienced many mistakes and wrongs by this time. But very soon I began to realize that Glen and I were establishing a strong friendship. He was very open to someone realizing some positive accomplishments and traits in him, which I could immediately see many. He was always ready to go to work on time and earlier; no one ever had to show him anything twice, or remind him to do something. He would do much on his own with no one asking him or pointing jobs out to him.

Eventually, he began to open up to me about all of his family problems and finally got around to the story about the reform school. He told me he was afraid to mention it because he thought I would hold it against him or even fire him if I knew about it. And all in all we began to have some very warm and heart to heart talks. Another thing that I think made quite an effect on it all was the fact that we were working really hard and steady, which lends a great atmosphere for people to find themselves. I had been told and believe it's true that to really get to know someone you should work along side of them on a job when you both have to sweat a lot for that is where a person's true nature comes out.

During one of our deep talks Glen told me one day that out of all of the miles of fence that he had seen in his life along railroads and highways and on the country side, it had never occurred to him what it took to build them. And now that we were doing this fencing, he knew how hard it was to dig post holes, put in braces, stretch wires, and build gates. It all took a lot of time, effort, and no-how. It seemed to be a huge realization to him that that is the way with most things. He would walk new areas of fence we had built in the last couple of days and admire the job and was very proud of the feeling of accomplishment.

At times he would talk about his days in the reform school and the kids he met there. He had already realized that he might have been better off to have never known some of them and once in a while realized there would be one he would worry about and wonder what might have happened to him.

He tried to reason with himself about the psychiatrist woman and what was her thinking. He would pace around and wrinkle up his face and yell, "Why? Why?" "That's all she would ever say to me," he would say. He could never figure out how he was supposed to answer her or what she was trying to teach him.

He had learned to take a piece of baling wire and short

across a car battery to get it real hot and light a cigarette. He'd remove a gas cap on a car and lightly press his nose in the filler hole and sniff gas until he would hallucinate; he said that would give him the worst headaches. We covered a lot of subjects and I tried to offer my feelings and advice and soon decided he had been down some roads I never even knew existed. But at the time, it seemed to me he was getting rid of a lot of pressure and ill feelings. I hoped that maybe he'd realize that some people around wouldn't judge him nearly as harshly as he had been used to.

After he had received a little money from his wages, he got to buying different kinds of models, including cars, trucks, and airplanes along with some buggies and horse drawn wagons. At night, in his sheep wagon, he would put them together and paint them. They were absolutely beautiful and his workmanship was detailed and flawless. Whatever the models were, they were priceless. He was very proud of them. To me, it showed his concentration and ability to do many things. On a couple of occasions he tried to give some of them to me, and I told him I was grateful. But I wanted him to keep them with his others, as I thought he should have them to show off his work to other people in case he wanted to impress someone with his efforts. As time went by, I would end up being very sorry for turning him down.

I was most happy with the work we were getting done, and I felt like he was really progressing with the talks and conversations we would have. Not because of any advice or what he learned from me, but I really learned to like him and appreciate him. I believe he knew this and that's why he started to come out of his lost state and reach out to someone who understood his needs and wanted to be there for him.

We had spent about three months on finishing the first fence and spent one day hauling post and wire and all of our supplies over to the east side of the ranch so we could start on the other portion of fence we were to build. That Friday night Glen asked me if I would take him to Harlowton; he needed some things and would like to take the weekend off.

We agreed, and it was about a 35-mile trip into town and upon reaching Main Street, he asked me to just let him off down town on a street corner. I didn't really understand that, but I didn't want to interfere in his business so I did as he asked. We said goodbye and the last thing he said was, "I'll see you Monday morning back at the ranch." As I was driving out of town, I watched him as he walked up the street alone.

One of the topics we covered a little bit on a number of occasions during those first three months of work was about his dad. Glen would ask me if I could remember him and did I know him very well. I began to realize that he wanted to know something good about him. In reality, I didn't know him very well, as I was pretty young myself when I first met him. But I did realize that at that time I looked up to him as someone I could admire because he looked very much like a typical cowboy, and anyone who did, I really admired and naturally wanted to be just like him. I used to tell Glen how I looked up to his dad at that time and I'm sure, as I realized how much he was fishing to hear some more good things about him, that I may have painted a pretty good picture of him to Glen, but not really knowing if some of my opinions were really very accurate. I remembered noticing how Glen would listen to every word I would say, and, while he seemed to savor the stories, he would sort of develop a look like, "how could that be?" or "I've never heard anyone say that before." He was just exhibiting some uncertainty.

I sometimes would want to ask him about his dad just to hear his opinion of him, but then he would change the subject. I was afraid to inquire as I felt he had darn sure been through enough explaining his problems to somebody. I felt his hearing and seeing some approval for a change was the best medicine for Glen. I never realized that some of the things I said to try and help Glen in our talks might one day really come back to haunt me. While my intentions were good, my information just might not have been completely true. But at this time, I didn't know. I hoped some positive approach might be worth something. I was somehow a little concerned about Glen's trip to town. I hoped he would be okay and not get into any trouble or have a hard time with his mother and his stepdad.

Saturday and Sunday rolled along and we had plenty to do at the ranch. One of the best things about being 40 miles out in the country on the ranch that you're trying to build and operate is that everything is quiet, pretty clear, and shielded from a lot of the trouble and goings on of the rest of the world. It's just about you, your family, your horses and cattle, and the weather. It is really pretty hard to beat, and I have to say it is my favorite place to be.

Monday morning came and livened up about 6:00am. I hadn't seen any sign of Glen yet, but I didn't think too much about it. It was just that I was used to him stepping out of that sheep wagon the instant he saw me doing chores at that hour, but this morning I figured he wasn't home yet. But after about 30 minutes of my ramming around out there, I noticed Glen standing in his wagon looking out the door. These sheep wagons have a split door on them, the top half and the bottom half. The bottom was shut, but the top half was open and he was standing back a little inside. I barely saw him standing there watching me through the top.

I could tell the minute I saw his actions that there was something wrong. I approached the wagon and, as I saw his face, I could see something very wrong. There was no smile and he spoke hardly any words. He waited to hear from me. I called out a good morning to him as cheerfully as I could and barely got an answer, but he did walk up closer to the door. He finally started to speak.

He started with an apology, and then a short statement about how much he liked working here and how badly he wanted that to continue. I told him that I felt the same way, but I said, "If something is wrong Glen, whatever it is, it's not going to change that." Then I said, "Let's have a seat and see what's gone wrong."

He just stepped up close to the door and said, "I guess I can say it best if I just show you." He unbuttoned his Levi's and slid them down, pulled up his T-shirt, and showed me a very nasty hernia. As he showed it to me, he explained that it had broken out on him a few days ago and was really hurting him, but he didn't want to say anything. That was when he decided he had better go see a doctor—hence the reason for our trip to town.

I told him he was totally right and that we better go

see about it. I would not want him to try to work with it, but no doubt we could get it fixed. He could come back out to the ranch to recuperate until he could work again. I tried to encourage him a little about being young, and that he would not doubt heal fast. But I knew in my heart it looked very bad to me, and I did not know anything at all about the seriousness of such a bad looking ailment as that. He ended up telling me that he had showed it to a doctor, and that they had told him to stop working and come in and get it worked on as soon as possible.

So we started preparations to load Glen and all of his possessions, models and all, and take him to town. Again, I tried to convey to him that he need not move away, that I would get him to a hospital, and then he would be more than welcome to come back and recover no matter how long it took or what might be necessary for us to do to make it all a success. We didn't even talk about how it might be paid for. But soon we were heading to town. On the way we talked a little about anything he might need, and whether he would like me to go see the doctor with him, and even if he would like me to enroll him in the hospital. But to all of these kinds of questions he very confidently convinced me that no, everything was under control.

Upon ending up in town, he asked me to drop him off downtown on a street corner. We spent a few, but very few, minutes saying goodbye and thanking each other for whatever either of us had done for the other. I promised him as quick as he had the chance to get his doctoring done, that I would be back to help him go on to his next move. He pretty much ended up telling me he thought he might go to visit some of his relatives. I sensed he needed to go on with his plans, so I drove away. The last I saw of him, he was standing on the street corner, all by himself.

The main thing I could remember thinking was that I wished that I knew what I should be saying to him if I was doing anything for him. But at last I arrived back home and went on with my own thoughts, problems, pleasant intentions, and accomplishments.

Before long, two weeks had passed and Glen was strong on my mind. It had started raining making it a little more difficult to work, so I finally decided I'd head into town and see if I could learn anything about Glen and how he was doing. We had no telephone out there and no mail service. Any contact with anyone else always started with making a trip to Martinsdale, which is where we got our mail, and at least there were telephones there so we could go that far and then do whatever was necessary from that point.

Upon reaching Martinsdale, I stopped and picked up the mail. There were no letters or word of any kind, so I was preparing to go on to Harlowton to locate Glen. In my stack of mail, I had received the latest Harlowton newspaper and started fanning through it. When I opened the paper, I sat staring at a picture and an article. It said that Glen had already had his funeral and that he died of a self-inflicted gunshot wound at the age of 17 years.

I could not hold my composure or even consider what to think and there was no one else there to say anything to. In trying to piece together what I could consider as having happened, it suddenly hit me. It was something he had said upon our saying good bye that day on the street in town. "I've been thinking I might go and visit some relatives." The only relative I knew of him having other than his mother was his dad. And I couldn't get over wondering if that was what he had meant.

After a little searching and remembering, I drove on back towards home. I wondered how such a young, precious, and prospective good human being could have so much tragedy and difficulties in his short life that could weigh so heavily on him to drive him to that kind of an end. How could I have failed to expect that or see it coming in our short span of time together? I had failed him. I thought of the time he tried to get me to take his models-I wish now that I had taken them. They probably ended up in someone's attic or possibly even the dump.

I wondered if he did not grasp the meaning of the stories I told to him about his Dad. Though well meaning, I sensed I might have caused him to lose credibility in what I told him. Although I truly believe to this day that there was nothing wrong with his Dad except that he had, through no fault of his own, missed some very important events in his son's growing up years. I know that as bad as I wanted to be there for him and wanted to see him do good, I had obviously let him down at the wrong time. I'm sure there were other people in his life who will never believe that I might have been able to help prevent such a wasted end. He still remains a person I will always be very pleased to have known though only for a short time.

I wish I knew for sure what all might take place in eternity.

CLIFFORD SHEARER STARTS OUT

Most people probably haven't ever had the opportunity to grow up in as nice a place as Ringling, Montana. It has large mountains with beautiful valleys and each with a pretty stream running down it full of fish. Cottonwood trees and all kinds of evergreens up in those high hills are native there and provide color, shade, and atmosphere to the area. One of the best things about the country is the big expanse of sagebrush which, when blooming in the Spring and the Fall, offers the best aroma anyone can hope to enjoy about the out of doors. It just fits Montana and with all of the different birds and wild life, it just doesn't leave anything left to your imagination. It is all right there; the Summers are short, and the Winters are long with deep and drifting snow packing into those sagebrush hills providing good moisture in the spring whenever 'mammy' nature decides to let Winter pass on out and Spring to ease in. It is sure good ranching country and that's about all that has ever gone on there in the line of industry.

At one point in history, the famous Ringling Brothers owned some ranching country there and used it to winter many of their circus animals. Near by was a large hot springs with hillsides of boiling mud and water that attracted people of all ages from all over the world who were afflicted with everything from stomach problems, arthritis, and skin disorders. Many left after bathing in the waters and mud banks feeling cured. Some felt relief, some felt helped, and some felt nothing at all. But they came and often returned. The settlers and families who came to Ringling and bought ranches or some other business usually stayed and lived out their lives there as did their kids and their grandchildren. And so it was. They were people who loved the land and made their living off that land.

Clifford Shearer's folks had both been born in Ringling and had grown up on ranches. When they met and got married, they went into business for themselves. They had a family and Clifford was their oldest. He grew up there realizing the many happy times and experiences that came from growing up on a Montana ranch with all that it had to offer. Good horses and cattle, some farming, good neighbors who worked with each other, and a real good cross section of summering and wintering; surviving both for yourself, the livestock, and the property you were responsible for. He and his very best friend, Roy, whose family were neighbors of the Shearers, had grown up together and spent 90 percent of their young lives riding their horses all over the countryside. They rode them when they went to town, when they went to work for the neighbors helping with brandings, roundups and such, when they were just scouting around the country, and even rode them to school. The two boys grew up like brothers and learned everything they knew together.

Then, as they started into the 8th grade, along came the Great Depression of 1929. They began to realize that life could get very difficult and what it was like to have absolutely nothing. Besides the break down in the economy, the country went into what became known as the 'dirty thirties' or the 'dust bowl days'. There were no jobs, no money, no industry, no market for any farm or ranch commodities like hay, grain, sheep or cattle. Even if there was a need for any of these things, there was not one person who could afford to buy any of it. No one could get a job because there was no market for any of the things that came from the land. People were starving, trying to flee the country, and some even committing suicide. Times became exceptionally down. People hoped that the country would soon recover—but it didn't happen. The breakdown went on for several years, until the government started to rebuild the whole economic system. The problem spread clear across America affecting the stock market, private business, and all industry, both large and small. Times were so bad that some people who tried to ship their calves or lambs to market ended up receiving a bill for freight that cost more than what their entire year's crop brought in and were unable to meet the payment. In those days it was pretty common to send their livestock to Chicago, or Omaha, yet even those large markets had no market at all. Everyone in the entire U.S. became destitute.

But back in Ringling, Montana, Clifford and Roy were toughing it out going through their eighth grade. Knowing that school was getting close to ending for the summer, the boys decided they should leave home and try to look for work. They knew that by staying at home, they were just one more mouth to feed for their parents, which meant just that much less food for their little brothers and sisters. It also occurred to them that if they could make some money, they could contribute to their parents' income and help them out a lot.

What the two of then didn't know then was that there were millions of working people who felt exactly the same way, but there were no jobs. They just supposed because they were young and innocent, that if they looked for work, they would find work. They had found an ad in some newspaper about a sawmill somewhere in Iowa that was hiring. It didn't mention wages, working conditions, or much about the job—only that they needed men. The two boys guarded their find feeling they were very lucky to have noticed the ad; it seemed like it was meant just for them as no one else ever mentioned it. They both knew that for their ages, they had done all types of jobs, and sure enough knew how to work. Neither of them had ever had any experience working in a sawmill, but they talked it all over and decided it would be good for them, and they could handle it regardless of what it took. Roy was a pretty good-sized boy. Clifford was small and frail, but only on the outside. Clifford was blessed with great determination, big ideas, and a lot of drive, and no amount of work or effort scared him at all.

Their biggest problem was getting the idea okayed by their parents. One night after they got home from school, they each told their folks of their plan. Clifford's dad listened to him and didn't say too much either way, which Clifford decided was a pretty probable okay, and he was surprised that maybe it wasn't going to be as tough as he had expected. But his mother was very different. She became upset and worried and did not like anything about the idea. She still saw Clifford as her little son who needed her, needed to be at home to grow up, and needed to go on to more schooling. But he hugged her and explained how much he wanted to help their income and relieve their pressures of running the household through these tough times. After a week or two of these discussions, he figured he could see them going for his idea. Each time the subject came up, Clifford noticed that his dad would start to talk to him in a real fatherly way, but would just stop—never saying what was on his mind. Clifford was anxious to hear his advice and would wait and listen for him to speak, but each time his dad would just find something else to do. He realized his dad was holding back some message that he really wanted to tell his son. Clifford was scared of the days ahead and of his new plan. He really wanted to hear his father's message, but between the two of them there was something that was not getting said. During this whole time there was a definite understanding between the father, mother, and son that there was a very strong love and dedication. Clifford did much soul searching alone and realized how much his parents, little brothers and sisters, and his home meant to him. They had brought him up right and he had a very good set of values. But he knew he must not weaken and must do what he felt he had to do.

In just another couple of days the two boys were looking at tomorrow being the last day of school. They both had their final arrangements made and decided that the next morning, after school let out, they would go into Ringling and catch a freight train headed east. They had played on the trains often, catching them, and riding them a couple of miles out of town, knowing the train would slow down, or even stop for a siding, where they would jump off and walk back into town. They felt quite comfortable riding the boxcar, knew the trains would get them into Iowa, but they weren't sure where this sawmill might be. They would worry about that when they arrived in the area.

Both their parents had consented to them leaving and the boys felt the sooner they started out, the better off the whole deal would work. They were both quite excited and pretty scared—but mostly optimistic. Clifford's Dad had told him that he would give him a ride into Ringling to the depot with the team and wagon. That made Clifford feel good as he figured he and his father could have that one last talk and make sure there were no hard feelings about his leaving home. He had known some other boys who had tried to leave and it had caused some real hard feelings with their parents for a long time. Clifford was very careful not to have this be the case between him and his parents.

The next two nights were spent making preparations for his leaving. Clifford still searched for that something he knew his Dad wanted to say to him, but neither night was the subject ever brought up, and then it was the morning for them to leave. Clifford's whole family crowded into the wagon to make the trip; his mother had packed him a lunch of all homemade goodies. His parents sat on the seat while Clifford and his brothers and sisters gathered in the wagon bed. There was some conversation at times but quite a lot of silence. All at once, about a quarter of a mile from the edge of town, the team was swinging along at a nice little trot when Clifford's father hauled back on the reins and hollered, "whoa!" The team slid to a stop and stood perfectly still. His dad turned around on the seat and was almost face to face with Clifford, and he said, "Clifford, I have many things I want to say to you, but, most of all, I wish everything about your leaving today was under much different circumstances. I am very proud of you." He stopped for a second, swallowed hard, and then went on. "I guess the one thing I really want you to know is this—don't ever get the idea that anybody owes you anything." He stopped and said no more as Clifford stared at him and tried to comprehend what he had just heard him say. They looked deep into each other's eyes, and before Clifford could even think of anything to say, his Dad turned around and clucked to the team. They got right back into their trot and, in a few moments, pulled up at the depot. When they arrived, Roy was already there and they could see the big steam engine in the distance bearing down upon them. Clifford and his parents jumped down from the wagon, hugged each of his little brothers and sisters, and turned and shook his father's hand. His father embraced him and said not a word. Clifford turned to hug his mother again and both of them cried hard; her tears landing on top of his head, running down his face, and his tears staining the plain, pale, little blue housedress she was wearing. He thanked her, she said nothing, and then he turned and ran to catch his train. She watched him run across the landing to the train and, because she was a mother, knew it would be a long, long time until she would see him again; he was going to look and be a lot different whenever that might happen. In seconds, the steam whistle sounded, the train jerked with each car, and the boys were stepping out into the big world to start life all on their own.

As they looked out from inside the boxcar door, they could see all the old familiar sights of Ringling, Montana, disappearing in the distance, their parents turning their wagons around, and each heading back out to their ranch. It was a day they really never thought they'd ever see.

They watched the countryside slide by as on into the day they traveled, not really knowing where they might be at any given moment. Darkness finally fell upon the land as town after town passed them by. They had eaten a little of Clifford's lunch and then tried to sleep. Clifford felt like many of the little colts and calves he had helped to wean from their mothers in his past years and knew he was feeling much like they had acted. He consoled himself with the fact that many times he had watched them be very upset for a few hours or maybe a night. He'd see them come into their own with their individual characteristics and dispositions, and he felt like that was how it would be with him. But as he lay on his coats in the boxcar, swinging and swaying, and trying to fall asleep, he kept thinking about what his father had said to him. "Don't ever get the idea that anybody owes you anything." He was sure it was a very important message, but he just could not figure out what it meant. He was just starting to find out that he would think about those words many, many times, and it would be a long time before he could one day say, "now I know what my dad was trying to tell me."

At last the boys arrived in a little town not too far from where their new job supposedly waited for them, soon they were walking through the gates and looking for the man named Jerry, who was the owner. He was pretty disappointed when he met the boys and was not at all impressed by them; he felt that they were pretty young and small for what he needed. But after looking them over and expressing disappointment in them, he told them both to follow him and they would be working the green chain. That is, carrying away the first cuts of every log, which means cutting it off on all four sides until it is squared up enough to start sawing dimension lumber from the tree. It is very hard and dirty work even for a grown and mature man. He had shown them just the barest of guidelines; staying out of the sawmill, staying away from flying bark and sticks are the most common hazards. He went back to his own position and left them to go to work. They were going to earn 60 cents per day each. The other thing they discovered was that Iowa was not experiencing the same drought as Montana. It was rainy and it rained hard every day—they were wading in mud knee-deep—no slickers, no overshoes, no rubber boots. All they had were their old farmer shoes they were wearing. Every day their feet were soaked and it was plain they would totally ruin their shoes in a very short time. After the first week they tried to get some money but couldn't—they were destitute. Jerry had no problem telling them he could not pay them until someone bought some lumber. He didn't even hardly have time to say he was sorry. He just said, "there's no money today." They did realize that Iowa was experiencing the same Depression. They finally traded for a place to stay and a little bit of groceries from a local store.

But into the second week, Roy became friends with a family from several hundred miles away, who took a liking to him and had some cows to milk. So he told Clifford goodbye and said they would all look for a better job for him and then left. Clifford was now doing both jobs. This went on and on. Sometimes he could get some money, many times he couldn't, but he hung on to what he got. Jerry was a mean and demanding boss and had no regard at all for Clifford. He mentioned almost daily that Clifford was poor help because he was inexperienced and too small. Clifford was on the verge of getting sick from working so hard. He realized, experienced or not, you didn't have to be real smart to do what he was doing. You had to be very tough, very stubborn, and very ambitious—he was all three—or he would have been gone the first day on the job. But he persisted, and he met people.

Finally, after what seemed like an eternity, Clifford realized it was September, and the kids he had grown up with would be starting school again back in Ringling. He felt quite left out, sick and disappointed as he thought of them, and of Roy, someplace else with a successful family on a big job. He was still no place at all, working on a lowly sawmill for almost no money that he could hardly ever collect, and he did not know what he should do. But he knew he was not a quitter, and so he would keep going.

Almost every night since he had left home, as he was falling asleep, he thought and thought about the last words his father said to him, "Don't ever get the idea that anybody owes you anything." Right at this particular time for him, he was more confused than he'd ever been about what his father had meant. He walked down to the sawmill for work this morning and found that the gates were locked. The mill was closed, and Jerry was nowhere to be found. Clifford was very disappointed he didn't have his job any longer. The owner had left with no warning or explanation and damn sure had not bothered to pay him. Clifford, for the first time in his life, was devastated.

At first there were individuals and families who had come to know him and took him in, but Clifford knew it was very tough on them and when he could, he worked for them. When there was no work, he went until he found something that needed doing. He moved around a little and tried a lot of jobs.

One morning he ran across an old man whom he had

met at the mill. He owned and operated a pretty substantial feedlot. He told Clifford to move out to his place as he could use some help and that's just what Clifford did.

It wasn't very long until the old man was teaching him a lot about feeder cattle, feeding cattle feeds, and the entire feedlot business. He and Clifford grew very close because Clifford became deeply interested, was a very attentive listener, and worked day and night. His time was spent mostly rebuilding and preparing the feed yard for a day in the future when they could restock and go back to feeding again. He also put up a lot of hay and harvested some grain the old man was raising. He could drive any team, and could do what ever needed to be done. Clifford felt that he had found the perfect place; the old man felt he had found the perfect young man. He had no one of his own and was very grateful for this youth he had found to train and lean on. It didn't seem to take very long before they realized Clifford had been there over a year.

The government had organized what had become known as the CCC Corps and offered jobs to people who could qualify to work for wages, which Clifford did, and then he would return to the old man's feedlot and do more work. This went on a little longer until they had enough money to buy their first load of feeder cattle and once again started the business the old man had been in his entire life but had been forced to close because of the Depression. Clifford was happy to be back among cattle and farming again after all of his adventures. Another year or two went on and Clifford had definitely found his new life's work. He became very seasoned and knowledgeable and the old man turned more and more over to him. Clifford went with him to the stock yards, and learned to buy; he bought feeds they needed and learned to sell some of what they raised. He learned about medicines, sickness, dealing with fat cattle buyers, trucking, shrink, and weighing conditions. Whatever was involved in the world of feeding cattle, Clifford learned to deal with. He had run into and been taught by one of the best people he could ever have started out with. He'd become a young man with an older man's foresight, knowledge, and experience. He never got much bigger physically, but gained enormously mentally and mechanically.

One evening as Clifford was winding up his evening chores, he saw a sheriff's car drive into their driveway. As soon as he had a chance, he went to see what was going on—he couldn't see the old man anyplace. The deputy, after asking Clifford a few questions and determining who he was, removed his hat and quietly told Clifford that his old partner had passed away in a pen of cattle at the sale barn that day in town. All he could say was that he must have died very happy as he was found in the middle of a herd of big feeder steer, which was the most important thing in his whole life. The deputy had said that a corral full of cattle meant more to that old fellow than if he had been sitting in his own living room. Clifford knew that was the absolute truth. It also went without saying that the old man had passed on almost everything he had ever learned in his life to Clifford.

The next thing they discussed was that the old fellow had left his entire life's holdings to Clifford. He had no one else. Times slowly got better for Clifford. He stayed on with his feedlot and began to put together some wealth.

He was pleased, happy, and felt quite successful; but after a while he began to think back about his childhood and Ringling, Montana. Times were much better than when he came to this Iowa country, but they were changing some. He felt that since his old partner had left him, he didn't feel as good about the feedlot business as he had at first. He thought more and more about his old home, the large expanse of land, and the raising of these cattle out in the wild Montana pasture country. He thought often of his dad and mother and brothers and sisters and realized he had not stayed in contact with them at all. He knew it had been nearly ten years since he had left home. One day, while talking to one of his neighbors, he mentioned his idea of selling his place to him and his two sons. He thought about it throughout the summer and decided that fall it was what he should do. By December the first, he was headed back home to his beloved old Montana—he had done very well for himself.

When he arrived home, he found once again there was another crisis. His brothers and sisters were grown and gone, his mother was living in White Sulphur Springs, and his father had passed away. Not much looked like he had remembered it, but he had a wonderful overdue reunion with his mother and old friends. Another crisis brought on by a guy named Adolph Hitler who was terrorizing the world and causing unheard of problems; it looked like all young men might have to go into the army and fight for their country,

Clifford ended up one of the first to volunteer, and was eventually followed by almost all of his old friends. Soon World War II was in full swing and Clifford saw much of a world he had never expected he would ever see. He became more experienced, older, wiser, and more matured. He learned much about life, death, camaraderie, hard times, and using his own scruples and ambitions. Finally it was over and he was on a troop train pulling once again back into Ringling, Montana. He thought again of the words his father had said to him back when he was a small boy. It seemed like a very long time ago. He had slaved at a sawmill, worked and worried in a feed yard, talked endlessly with his best friend at that time, and later slept and hovered in fox holes with guns and bombs going off everywhere all around him. It was very peaceful coming home from all of that and the age-old question confronted him again, but he couldn't really say he had yet figured out the answer.

About as soon as Clifford got back home and caught his breath again, he bought a nice ranch in the hill country to the south and west of Ringling. He stocked it with good cattle and horses, married a really nice girl, and raised a family of his own. He eventually shifted his herd of cattle to Charlais and became very well known for his good calves and even sold many of his neighbors' breeding heifers and bulls. As the years went along, Clifford became very successful. Not only financially but just as a human being.

He persisted for several decades there and enjoyed a life style that not all people get to experience. One warm summer evening quite late at night, I ran into Clifford in the Stockman's bar in White Sulphur Springs and after having set and visited and partaken of a few bottles of beer, Clifford told a little group of us people who were all younger than him a few of the highlights of this very story. We all sat spellbound waiting to hear the rest of the story, but wishing it would not end.

Clifford pushed his hat back and staring through his glasses, he looked way out there past all of us and he said, "you know now I am 71 years old, and I think maybe I'm beginning to get a pretty good idea of what my Dad was trying to tell me. But I know it helped me to get through all that I did and end up where I am today.

It is my personal belief that he spent working his entire life based on the advice of his father that could be good for almost every one of us.

"Don't ever get the idea that anybody owes you anything!"

A REAL GOOD LESSON

For all of my growing up years, starting back in my high school days, I have been involved in buying, selling, and riding horses. Horses have always been a huge magnet for me, and I can't say it much better than to say I see them as the most remarkable and amazing animal of all of God's creations.

In the beginning I only saw them as a source of income

and a source of security that would lead me into whatever future I might want to have. Of all the experiences I have had in my life that I can remember after 60 years of my associations involving horses, I see something else. I see all that they have taught me and how they have shaped my thinking, my attitude, and my expectations about every aspect of life. Horses are the greatest friends, providers of life lessons, and one of the greatest assets there is on earth next to having good health.

It took some time to come to view seeing horses as more than just a source of income. Over the years I have derived so much pleasure from them on one hand, and on the other hand, I have difficulty being able to forgive myself for the times I know I let them down because of my inadequacies or misguided opinions of some detail. I realize now with regret, that I completely wasted some horses' opportunities, and probably led to the total destruction of others.

My personal trail I've traveled on in the world of horses, along with my wife, took us around the country going to many different ranches and horse sales and answering advertisements for horses for sale. I came to the conclusion along the way that we were ending up buying a lot of problem horses. We trustingly believed sellers' stories about the conditions and training of a lot of the horses, and after we had paid for them and got them home, realized that we had missed a lot of things. We ended up with some horses that were not very saleable because of their faults. It occurred to us that if we went into the business of raising our own horses, we would know their complete history and breeding instead of taking some unknown person's word about the horses we would acquire. My wife and I worked it out with paper and pencil and realized that raising our own horses would cost us much less than we were spending on traveling to sales for acquiring horses.

This new idea came about happening quite easily and we enjoyed quite a bit of good luck at times. We acquired a really nice pasture and quickly built up to 30 head of mares that we basically hand picked. We even bought a 3-year-old stallion, which a good friend of ours had sent us to break for him. That was when my education about horses really began.

I watched as each new baby horse came into the world, saw them stand for the first time, take their first breath, see their surroundings for the first time, and meet its own mother face to face. With each new birth I witnessed, I learned lessons that can not be learned any other way.

The same holds true, that you have to see it for yourself, watching those same babies survive the summer weaning's, halter breaking, branding, one year old birthday's, two year old birthday's, and finally becoming broke to ride. While all of this was happening, I also realized that the new ones being born needed the same things, and I hoped I could improve on the care and maintenance with each new crop. Placing and selling each year's babies ready for sale, updating bloodlines by adding to the stallion's in our breeding operation were all part of the learning process. I spent a lot of time learning the hard way about doctoring, shoeing, breeding, and culling the bloodlines in an effort to improve on our product.

Through all of these experiences eventually came the

realization that each one of these parcels is an individual, with their own peculiarities and differences and feelings. Not very often are any two animals alike, other than they are all identifiable as belonging to the same horse family.

I contacted trainers, feed authorities, other owner/breeders, teachers, and participated in clinics, and listened to countless opinions in order to learn. Some opinions were of much value, but occasionally some were pretty poor information. No matter what the information, I always arrived at the same conclusion that there was much still left to learn, and for sure not a long enough life span to ever stop trying to learn it all.

Eventually, the pendulum of the economy started to swing away from prosperity. This shift brought along drought and the scarcity of pasture, and we had to scale back our operation. We had to divide up the band of mares that we were very proud of, that we had so painstakingly put together, and we watched them scatter to the winds. Many of these mares we had bred and raised ourselves. With each one of the mares leaving us—so went the product I had been trying to create and improve upon. I could see as each mare dropped out of our circle and was sold to someone different, there was the possibility that new person wouldn't know, or even notice the horses individual attributes, and that she could end up just another horse in a little pen. I realized how the mares' lives could be wasted by someone not seeing the horses as individuals instead of product, and what a gross injustice it was to that individual horse and the horse species in general.

It is the plain truth that there are great champions

in the show rings of the world, breeding barns and on ranches that very well meaning and highly knowledge-able people have spent many thousands of dollars on, advertising in order to establish accolades for their horses. It is a sad, plain truth that thousands of other horses have been damaged, passed over, and/or sacrificed in order to create those accolades and champions.

Approximately 30 years ago we started a monthly horse auction here at our ranch. In the scheme of things it is very small scale operation and insignificant to the rest of the horse world, but I sure feel that it's given me more insight into the individual rights and consideration of each and every horse. Once a month we take the horses that come to our sale and try to determine in a couple of minutes each horse's individual worth and what to say about his repu-tation. There have been times when it honestly looked like the horse's future would be an improvement of some sort from its present circumstance, but in many other cases the horse only could look forward to a pretty dismal step or two backwards, depending on who purchased the animal. In each case, as a horse would step forward to learn his fate, he complained not at all and just silently accepted it. I could certainly see in his or her intelligent eyes that nothing was escaping his notice, whether it may be a future for the better or for the worse.

It seems some of the best stories we see happen are centered around kids, and how they become responsible and claim ownership of a horse. In most cases, kids seek out trainers who can help them to understand what the horse is all about. Then the horse himself teaches the young person, and they learn good communication, responsibility and many wide reaching lesson's about life during their daily caring for and spending time with that horse.

One of my favorite stories along these lines took place here at one of our sale's about 7 or 8 years ago. It was the December sale, sometimes referred to as our Christmas sale. We had ponies and many different classes of horses we knew were coming in. The sale went quite well.

Among the crowd were three young guys who were very excited because they had bought out an old experienced canner horse buyer and were just now embarking on their new path to fame and fortune as canner buyers. A canner buyer purchases horses at auction for slaughter. These three were buying every horse they could and, at the same time, celebrating their new business along with a side of Christmas cheer. Consequently, they got a little out of touch with the reasonable value of some of these older and more used up horses they had come to buy. As the day wore on they became more generous in their bids, and they lost track of how many they were buying.

Some consigner from out in the hills had brought in an old buckskin mare to be sold. The mare looked very old and used up. She hadn't been wormed or groomed in several years and her feet were in tough condition. The old mare had wrinkles in her face and eyes that made me think she was at least close to 30-years-old, and had not benefited from regular feed. She looked really bad. She made it into the sale ring and was bought by our newest canner buyers-the three full of Christmas cheer. I'm not real sure if she was even conscious of what was going on, and she went back to her pen appearing pretty oblivious to all that was happening.

When the sale had ended and the business of settling up bills and squeezing the days purchases into inadequate trailers was done, the old buckskin mare had been over looked and totally forgotten about. We were grateful she had been forgotten, and intentionally did not mention her to them. We were very concerned about them cramming her onto the trailer, realizing she would end up trampled on the floor of the already over loaded trailer. When the buyers had gone from the sale, the old mare stood abandoned and forgotten alone in her pen. At least the pen was clean and dry, had a roof on it. And she had feed and water.

With them leaving her behind, we became the proud owners of her. She had been sold at their inflated Christmas cheer purchase price, and the consignor had already collected his check and had gone home also. I began to wonder what I would ever be able to do with her. The next day was a Sunday, and at 6:00 o'clock in the morning the phone rang. There was a very earnest sounding female voice on the other end stating that she had been to the sale Saturday and had spotted this old buckskin mare but she hadn't been able to stay at the sale very long. Her question so early that morning was, "Do you remember the horse?" The caller wanted to know whether or not the mare had been sold or if there was a chance she might still be able to buy her. I answered that "yes" she was still here and that caller could buy her. The caller went on to say that she had $450 that she could give for her. I merely said that will work.

I thought I could remember this lady from some past dealings, and it seemed to me I remembered she was a very well meaning person. As a horseman or judge of a horse though, I thought she left a lot to be desired. We left the conversation that morning with her saying that she'd be by to pay for the mare, but that she would like to leave her for 3 or 4 days before she picked her up, which was all totally agreeable by me.

I don't consider myself as any kind of authority, and I don't judge everyone and their motives, but I wondered what plan she could possibly have for that very old and used up mare I saw. I also wondered whether that mare would in fact live for the next three or fours days until the lady came to pick her up.

The day before Christmas, the woman who had called drove into our yard to pick up her mare, explaining how she had needed the time to work fixing up a nice pen for the mare. She wanted to have everything ready for the mare. The woman was slightly apprehensive as she examined and scrutinized her new mare, but all she said was she hoped she wasn't making a mistake as we loaded the mare into the trailer. As we loaded the mare, I swear I saw a new enthusiasm emerging from the both of them. As the lady was driving away she said out the window I hope what I see here in this mare is real.

All I could say to myself as she drove away was I'm glad this poor little mare has finally found a little respect and care that I'm sure she deserves. Things were busy and I had to turn to something a little more pressing, and I forgot about the mare.

About a week after Christmas, the lady came to my house again. As we greeted each other and sat down to talk, I was expecting to hear a bad story about changing her mind or worse. She handed me an envelope and looking inside, I saw a neatly written message, which contained one of the neatest stories that I could have ever imagined. First thing I noticed inside the envelope was a color picture of a very attractive buckskin horse. The picture showed a very shiny and groomed horse, with a huge dark eye and happy expression. I admired that picture for a second and then started reading the note. The note was from the lady and said that knew this little girl who is 9 years old and lives down the street from her. The little girl used to have an old gelding. Every single day of her life the little girl rode him bareback, fed him, groomed him and cared for him. The girl had little time or interest in doing anything else but spending time with her horse. One morning about a month ago, the little girl went out to care for her horse, and she realized he did not meet her at the back gate like he usually did. She found him dead in the back of his little pasture. His time had simply run out.

The note went on to say how the little girl was so devastated that she was having trouble functioning. When the woman had seen the little buckskin mare at the sale, she could see that the mare and that little girl could be good medicine for each other. The note said how now they both have a new purpose, and that little girl is back riding again on her new horse, with a nice new saddle her folks had given her. The little girl and the mare are both enjoying a brand new beginning. The mare was perfect for the little girl and as you can see from the photograph, she has an entirely different look and attitude.

In the note, the lady went on to thank me for helping her to find the mare. I felt this thanks was completely out of place. The lady was the one who had the foresight to see what was actually standing on those four legs that day at our horse sale. It was all totally missed by me.

It was very obvious the happiness the lady received from seeing both the mare and the little girl becoming a perfect pair. The lady, the little girl, and the mare, all gaining something from what they were giving, and enjoying each other every day.

This example of the true value of a horse, without the ingredient of money or dollars and cents involved, was one of the biggest lesson's I've learned of all. I needed to remember to look past the dim and dismal picture I saw, and ask why did I not see all of that possibility instead. When I saw the little girl with her huge smile and bright eyes riding around the arena at their own speed, they both had the identical look of happiness on their face's.

All of these people—the lady with the good heart, the little girl who was so deserving of the lady's good deed, and even the little buckskin mare, were all created by the same God who sees all and misses nothing. He also provides us with lessons. All of the events that entered into the final disposition of the buckskin mare coming to our auction to be sold, being completely forgotten by the canner buyer, and then having the lady find her there at the sale so the mare could end up with the little girl for a life filled with happiness, healing and enjoyment, was a plan truly laid out and handled by a very caring Almighty God.

I have come a long way in my thinking over the years, from a horse being a product, to seeing them as individual creations of God. No one ever will know what had been in the buckskin mares past, but it was clear that God knew what needed to be done, not only to help the little girl and the mare, but also to show me again the value of the relationship between horses and people.

BILL AND
MOLLY

In September of 1946, one sunny Saturday morning, my Dad loaded my brother and me up in the pickup, and we all went to a little ranch about five miles east and south of Harlowton to an auction sale. I believe it was the first one I had ever been to, and was the sale of an old timer in the Harlowton area by the name of Charlie Beachot (pronounced like Berchey). The auctioneer was a very well known man, cattle buyer, and figure in the area by the name of W. J. Tucker.

I was just ten-years-old, and I knew that horses, ranches, and all of the related subjects were of extreme interest to me. My Dad hadn't said much to me about where we were going that morning, he had just told us to get ready and we went. When we got there, it was just all happening and I found more excitement than I had ever known, or ever expected. But I was sure on hand to take in everything that was going on, and I was really taken in with listening to old Tucker's bid calling. He was really a fine auctioneer and very good man.

I watched without missing one single thing as machinery, sheep, a few household items, lots of tools, sheep panels, lambing jugs, and almost everything else ever found on a ranch in Montana was sold on that eventful day. Finally, as the sale was getting down towards the end, a nice big team of bay horses was led up before the crowd.

Old Tucker stopped his chanting and stood back, maybe making a small joke with someone in the crowd. The two big horses crowded against each other, a little bewildered, stood up and looked over first one way, and then another, eventually taking in every one of all of the friends, neighbors, and bidders who had come to help old Charlie dispose of his worldly belongings. Finally, as they began to settle down just a little, the auctioneer said to old man Beachot, "All right Charlie, can you tell us the story on the team?" Old Charlie in his old man's voice said; "Boys, I have owned these horses since they were three-year-olds. I bought them over around Bozeman, just after they were broke. They have been together their whole lives as they were raised together from baby colts. Broke out right there on the same ranch at two-years-old, and I bought them the next year at three, and have had them ever since. The mare is a little faster than the gelding, and she works on the right. I would put them up against any team in the country. They are plumb gentle, easy to catch, good pullers, and they're exactly fifteen-years-old." Someone in the crowd asked him what they would weigh, and he answered, "Around fifteen hundred pounds a piece."

With that, the men leading each one of them turned them around a time or two as old Tucker gave a short speech about their good points and said, "We'll sell them together along with the harness they have on—and what will you give for the team and the harness?" The bidding started and went on for a few minutes. He stopped once more, talked about them one more time, went on with his bid calling for just a short time and said, "Sold, one hundred dollars to Buster Robertson." My head swung around, for as close as I was watching the whole thing, and I thought not missing anything, I realized all at once that my dad had just bought that team of horses, which to me was the most exciting thing at the whole sale! As the horses were led back to the corrals, I heard my dad ask old Charlie, "What do you call them?" "Bill and Molly," answered Charlie. I guess that was about the biggest thing I had seen happen in most of my young life.

In just a day or so, we had Bill and Molly home and were beginning to use them for all kinds of work. We had had teams around for a long time, and I loved them all very much and knew them all real well. We had a big grey horse called Amos, his mother, and an old grey mare we worked with him called Mabel. There was also an old bay mare called Nellie. But I guess both Nellie and Mabel had gotten old and pretty well wore out, and Dad had shipped them off to a horse sale in Billings. So, by the time Bill and Molly came along, there was a lot of work to catch up on. The war hadn't been over with that long, and all we had for any kind of a tractor was a little Model A Farmall, which was small enough that old Bill and Molly could work circles around it. Tractors were very hard to get, cost a lot of money, and burnt gasoline, which wasn't that plentiful. Our ranch was pretty small so a good team was the best solution yet for a few more years.

One of the first jobs we tried with the new team was cleaning the corrals, which consisted of their pulling a Fresno down through each one, over a bank, and would be dumped in a spot where the manure wouldn't be in anyone's way. It really wasn't such a tough pulling job, but gave Dad a chance to work the horses together and kind of get the feel of the team, and they, in turn, the feel of him and his way of handling them. As the days went on, there was fencing, wood hauling, and finally, the biggest wintertime job of all, hauling and feeding hay. We found the team to be exactly like old Charlie Beachot had described them at his sale that day. The mare was a little stockier than the gelding, was bay in color, had one white hind foot, and a big diamond shape in her forehead. Her mane and tail were black. She pulled on any load you hooked her up to just as hard as she possibly could and if it happened to be a little too much for her, she would back off and gather herself all up, really get down and lift on it, until there was just no way—it had to come with her. But in walking down a trail or out across country pulling a hay rack or high wheeled wagon, she was right up on the bit and you had to keep holding her down just a little. Old Bill was taller, pretty slim, and all bay in color with just a spot about the size of a silver dollar in his forehead. He, too, had a black mane and tail. But he traveled along at a nice easy gait, and never changed it a bit, or got excited about anything. If the load took a whole lot of extra pull, he just simply laid into his tugs a little harder and, again, there just wasn't much of anything within reason that he couldn't just walk away with. Together they were for sure a real team.

We were, at this time, in the dairy business, milking right at thirty cows morning and night, and we used to feed them in a big long line out of a hayrack. We had all loose hay at the time, used to haul a big load in each day, and feed the cows the night feed using about half of the load. Then we would give them the rest on the wagon the next morning. During the day we would go load it up again for that night's feed, repeating the whole process again the next day. In just no time at all, Bill and Molly learned their routine, and would walk around the feeding area without anyone even driving them. They knew just exactly where to go and how fast to travel. In time I got to drive them, and that was my first experience at driving a team.

As we kind of got on into the winter, the river would freeze over solid enough that we would cross it on the ice. Usually we would have to haul a load of manure out on the ice and make a trail for the horses to walk on. The ice alone would get so slick that the team could slip and sometimes fall, possibly hurting one of them or scaring them bad enough that they would be too afraid to cross the ice again. But they soon learned that when we made them a road out of manure, in no time at all, it would melt into the ice and get solid so they could walk right across with no problem. But in the course of the winter with its cold spells, then a week or two of warming, then another cold turn; sometimes water would run maybe as much as six or eight inches over the existing ice. After several of these occurrences, it would eventually get to where there might be a foot or more of drop off from the banks along the river down onto the ice. With a big load of hay on, a person would have to pull up real close and just ease down onto the ice, or if you hit it too hard, you could either spill a bunch of your hay off of the front of the load, or even sometimes you might break the wagon down. Bill and Molly got so they were really good at knowing just how to ease down on to that ice, but when they got to the other side, it would be like someone throwing a block in front of the wheels when they hit that high bank coming out. They got so they would start running, really hit it hard, and kind of bounced the hayrack up over it. This would give the wagon a hard jolt, and would sometimes either throw some hay off of the front, or tear up the wagon a little, and could even come darn near throwing the guy driving right off of the top of the load.

My oldest brother was by this time in his second year of high school. He used to haul an awful lot of hay either by himself or with one of us other two boys helping him. But he usually drove the team either way.

One very cold evening he was coming home with a load of hay on, and he got to the river. He went to ease down into it, as he knew he had to, but something went a little bit wrong, and the old team let the load get away from them, and dropped it a little too hard down onto the ice, and bounced Frank and quite a bit of the load right off of the front of the hayrack. Frank had really put on a high load and must have fallen at least twelve feet down right flat on his back on that ice. The fall alone was bad enough, but it just happened that the beavers had cut some willows off right there about four or five inches above the ice, and Frank hit right on top of one of these stumps and it went into his back.

When he was thrown off of the wagon, it left no one driving the team. They made their usual run on across the river until they made it up the bank on the other side, and I guess realized that something was wrong and they stopped. It took Frank quite a while to get himself moving again as he was pretty badly hurt. He finally managed to crawl across the ice and up on top of the bank. He had to crawl around that team, get his lines gathered up, and holding them, get himself back up on top of the load of hay and drove the team on home. He said it spooked the horses pretty bad, but they did not run away. By the time he got into the yard that night, he had to have help getting into the house. He sure suffered a lot of pain for a long time and it ended up crippling him for the rest of his life. He was eventually operated on for the injury several years later, and had the problem pretty well corrected, but he still suffers from it yet to this day. But it was really quite a spectacular thing that those two horses did not run away with that wagon and leave Frank laying back there hurting, as well as maybe tearing up the wagon or maybe even themselves.

As spring and summer came around, it became evident that old Bill was a real extravert. He would team up with any of the other horses on the ranch and seemed to be everybody's friend. But old Molly was a little sour around any of the other horses. She usually followed Bill around, and no matter where you would find them; she would always be on his right side. I have been told many times that you could always watch an old team that had worked together a lot, and tell which one worked on which side, as they would almost always line up that way even when they were just running loose out in the pasture. It was sure true with her. But I don't think Bill ever paid much attention, he just kind of left it up to her to keep that part straight. But Bill went out of his way to be a friend to all of the horses, while Molly just remained real loyal to only Bill. They had been through a lot, had made many miles, and even seen some changes together and she seemed to want to keep close to Bill at all times.

That summer we used Bill and Molly haying, both at home and helping the neighbors put up hay, and did quite a bit of thrashing with them in the fall. My Dad contracted to put up a lot of hay for a ranch that had been bought by some speculator about three miles from our place. The deal had taken place late in the summer, and none of the hay had been put up yet. We used the old team a lot both raking hay, and on the buck rake as this hay, too, was all put up loose.

After the haying was finished, Dad ended up buying part of the ranch, and that next winter we spent a lot of time on that place fencing and preparing to have it ready to stock come the next spring. He started making plans to sell our old home place after he was sure he had cleared the deal on the new place, and in the whole process, he decided to quit the dairy business.

That winter was an exceptionally bad one, with below normal cold temperatures, and above normal snowfall. Our road leading in and out of the old home place became plumb blocked for several months and Bill and Molly became our biggest mode of getting back and forth. The old team made many trips of three miles each way hauling hay, as well as other things we needed brought to the new ranch, every day for quite a long spell that winter. I also remember using them to pull the pickup quite a few mornings that winter trying to get it started, as we had to leave it parked out in the hills a half a mile or so from the house because of snowdrifts, and due to the extremely cold mornings, it would not start. Dad would hook Bill and Molly on to it and drag it around and around the flats out in those hills; the hind tires wouldn't even turn because the transmission would be so cold and stiff. After an hour or so of trying to start it, he would have to give up, and just drive the team to the other ranch to do his feeding, and to get us kids to school.

The cold winter had really taken a lot out of both man and beast by along towards the end of February, when at last a Chinook wind blew in warm and mighty welcome one night. For about a week the snows began to melt, and there was water running everywhere. But, of course, there was still the necessary feeding to be done. By this late in the winter, we were hauling hay from the north side of the ranch, which involved climbing some pretty steep hills, and the round trip added up to about a mile and a half every day. As always was the habit, we would feed the cattle each morning, then tend to all of the other chores, such as chopping water holes, straightening out any new problems that arose each day and then, when all of these things were done, someone would always take Bill and Molly out to the hay stack to load the hayrack again for the next morning. Another factor that determined this loading late in the afternoon was the fact that the wind often blew pretty strong all day making it real hard, and sometimes impossible, to pitch loose hay. But oftentimes by four or five o'clock in the afternoon, that wind would start to go down, and make it a better time to be out there loading the hay for tomorrow. So this one evening, about four in the afternoon, Dad started out to go get his load of hay. He told us about it later, as he talked of it many times, how he had climbed the steep hill onto the flat that led over to the hay meadow, and the team, knowing exactly what was to be done, struck up a pretty good little trot, just anxious to get the job done as Dad himself. He said they were sweating pretty good from the tough pull, and with the Chinook wind still blowing, the weather was pretty warm. He said he held them down a little, but old Molly, as usual, was leaning hard into the bit, and really pulling the biggest share of the wagon. Bill was trotting to keep up with her but, in his long easy stride, was just doing exactly that and not really pulling much of the wagon. Dad said that all of a sudden he noticed Molly kind of let up and almost stop, and then fell to her knees, and just pitched forward right onto her nose, before falling over on her side.

He got Bill stopped, jumped off of the hay rack, and ran up in front to the team to examine Molly. But he said she had already stopped breathing, and was lying very still. He hurried to unhook her, and tried to pull her harness off, but he realized his precious mare was dead. He finally got Bill unhooked and got the harness apart separating the two horses, led Bill back and tied him to the wagon. He examined Molly real good again, but he knew by now that she would never get up, and that her days were all over. He finally managed to get her harness off of her, hung it on the wagon, untied Bill, turned around, and started leading him back towards home. My Dad was a very sentimental person, but when it involved any of his animals he was especially so, and worse than ever about his horses. But as bad as he felt over seeing his beloved

Molly die in her harness working so very hard for him, he really felt the most for poor old Bill. He told us that when he tried to lead Bill away from the downed mare, he just kept stopping and turning around and stopping again to stare at her lying there right at her place at the front of that wagon where the two of them had made so many miles. Animals all do their suffering in silence, although when you get to know them, you can read their minds, and my Dad sure knew what all was going through old Bill's mind at that moment. He really didn't want to walk away from that hay wagon without his faithful old friend. She had been a part of him and every single thing he did for seventeen years. It was by now 1948 and we had owned Bill and Molly for going on two years.

Dad finally coaxed Bill on home, fed him, and turned him loose for the night. He headed right straight back out over the hill, and spent the night standing around Molly. The next morning Bill was nowhere in sight, and we finally found him out there standing beside Molly. When we brought him into the corrals, we went and dragged the old mare's body away. Bill stood and looked out over the fence all day, whinnied and nickered, and stared out over the hills as far as he could look. But she had died about half a mile from the ranch and was not in sight from the corrals. For several days, every time he was loose and running out side, Bill would go to that spot and stand where Molly had breathed her last. It was much the same as when you take a colt or a calf from its mother, the cow or mare, which ever the case might be, will go back to that spot, stand there, and bawl or whinny for several days. Slowly, the poor old gelding gave up and accepted his loss, but his spirit did not improve. He moped around, and acted very slow, almost as if he were sick. He did not care about any of the other horses; he just kept strictly to himself for days.

Finally, one day, Dad said, "I guess that better be enough, we have to get poor old Bill something else to think about. Lets get Amos in, and hook him up with Bill and see if they will work as a team." So that was what we did, and they worked together and, in a few days, made a pretty good team. But poor Bill could never get up much enthusiasm. And finally, one day, Dad found another workhorse to mate up with Amos, and he took Bill over to our new ranch and turned him out for a while.

We eventually got moved in to the new place, and sold the old home. While Bill and Molly were really not considered all that old at seventeen years, she had sure enough died, I guess of a heart attack, at an age where she really should have had at least ten more years of life yet to go. Not necessarily being able to work all of those years, but at least maybe putting in three or four more good years. And then she should have enjoyed about five or six years of retirement.

We kept Bill for a couple of years, and one day an old man stopped by the ranch and asked Dad about him. He said he had noticed the old horse standing along the road, and thought he looked like a pretty good horse and wondered if he would ever be for sale. Dad told the old fellow the whole story of Bill's life, and said that he considered Bill as being retired. The old man said that he had just a small place, and was trying to operate a little one-horse sawmill over in the Bozeman area and would sure like to have Bill for a skidding horse. He ended up telling Dad that he had a three-year-old palomino mare that would really make someone a nice saddle horse if they would take her and break her out. He said that he would trade her and fifty dollars for Bill. Dad finally agreed and, in a day or two, the man showed up again with his palomino mare, the fifty dollars, and they traded. The mare was everything he had told us she was, and eventually broke out and became an outstanding horse. She became about the first horse that I ever broke, and after a year, Dad gave her to me. I rode her for several years and, eventually, sold her to a very good friend of mine, who also lived in the Bozeman area. The old man took Bill to his ranch, used him for a year or two, and turned him out with some little colts that he was weaning. He told us that he retired the faithful old horse, using him just for that. He raised quite a few colts, and he said that every fall when he went to wean them, he liked to have a good gentle horse to run with them to help settle them down. He said that became Bill's job, and he also said that Bill became the best babysitter that he had ever had for that job. That was the last we ever heard of Bill. I never ever got to hear how many years he lasted at it, but I imagine it was about a stand off which one lasted out the other—the old horse or the old man. Neither one of them had too many years to go the last time I knew of them. The old man's name was Ben Birkey and he came from a long line of horsemen.

Often in remembering back, I can still see my dad driving Bill and Molly up across that flat to where that hay stack used to be; my dad with his pipe in his mouth, and that old Montana west wind blowing the smoke from that pipe back over his shoulder. Old Molly straining to go just a little faster than she needed to, and Bill easily swinging along beside her—kind of letting her go ahead and do a little more than her share if she really wanted to. I can hear the ringing and rattling of their harness and their trace chains, as well as the hammering and rattling of the big hay wagon they used to pull. For me it is pleasant to remember back, and to know that in that little area that was our old home place, there was once their tracks left in the dry dirt, the mud, and the past, while most certainly incidental, and of no importance to any one at all, it still remains their story, and it is much like those of a great many other horses just like them.

They were never famous for their size because, as workhorses go, they weren't real big. They didn't ever do anything involving any great or famous people, nor were hardly even known by any of our neighbors. They were just an old team of horses that belonged to first one, then another, and finally Bill to still another. But one thing for sure is that they didn't do anything but good for everyone who knew them.

A SUCCESSFUL COWMAN OF DAYS GONE PAST

There is a story that has been told many time over, of A.B. Cook—a very dedicated and successful cowman from the past. This successful cowman developed his ranching and cattle operation with great tenacity in the area I grew up, and many people held him in high esteem. Even after his death, folks from all around were fond of telling their memories and accounts of the man, his dream, and his accomplishments.

A.B. Cook had established a cattle ranch in the early days of the Townsen, Montana area. From all accounts, the ranch wasn't on a particularly fancy piece of ranch country; instead it was located in a dry, rocky, and barren area. A large lake was established in the area, that became known as Canyon Ferry, to bring much needed irrigation and improvement to that part of Montana's dry ranch land. For many years after the death of Mr. Cook, there were still large, old signs in the area, with painted pictures of Hereford cattle on them and advertising A.B. Cook Stock Farms. I used to think the use of the word "farms" was a little unusual for that part of the country, when it was quite common to call an enterprise that ran and raised beef cattle a ranch. In that area, the word "farm" referred more to a grain or food producing operation, and as a youth growing up there, I always found one would get corrected pretty quick if you called a cattle ranch a farm.

The way Mr. Cook's history was told to me, began with how he had started out as a young man trying to raise the cattle of the day, which were just bovine species. No one had attempted to upgrade or improve the performance of the cattle. The main thing the ranchers really looked for were cattle that were hearty enough to withstand hot, dry summers, long, cold, snowy winters, all with no abundance of feed, very little water, and no pampering. If there was some rain and some breaks in the weather, well, they might do just a little better than in other years. But after spending a portion of his younger years struggling along, barely making a living, he began to learn a more about his business and tried to upgrade his cattle. He realized that with a little effort on his part, it quite often produced much better results. He studied his lessons, read a lot, experimented, and soon became quite an authority on breeding and sources for the new breed called Hereford. As this all started to progress, A.B. focused himself on raising his son and daughter. While I expect he loved his family, he realized they had little interest in his ranch, the cattle, and what he was trying to do. He was somewhat frustrated and disappointed in them, as they were never going to be of much help to him with his improvements. But he continued on. The years ran on and they did crop after crop of his calves began to get quite popular to buyers from every corner of the United States.

Finally, as he labored more and more to build a better

breed of cattle and, in fact, reaped a lot of the rewards, he made a decision to go to the local bank and borrow quite a substantial amount of money to really step up his breeding program. By this time he was most definitely sold on what he was doing, but he had spent a big portion of his life getting to this point. He saw a huge improvement in the demand and receipts for his cattle, but, evidently, the bank did not share his enthusiasm. He had a lot of trouble trying to convince them in the beginning, but they slowly realized his dedication and success and loaned him some money. A.B. didn't get all that he needed but he did get a portion of what they felt he could get by with. He continued on at a considerably better rate, mostly because he used the borrowed money sparingly and wisely in upgrading his breeding bulls. Even the bank realized the demand for his calves and the influx of influential breeders and buyers from as far away as Texas and Georgia, and that Mr. Cook was not able to raise enough new calves each year to meet and fulfill his demand. They continued on supporting him and all enjoyed a very successful return.

After a couple of years of this partnership, I believe in the middle to late 1940s, they began to worry that the cow business was going to weaken. In the Fall, when Mr. Cook came in to settle up with them, he was planning to show how easily he could increase his operation and get more of a loan, strictly on the strength of a very successful year. The bank surprised him by ordering payment in full or what he could give them and the balance would be taken by foreclosure.

Mr. Cook was totally devastated. He could only see that they were cutting him off at his hip pockets and his entire program was going to end. But it was so ordered and they were going to order a dispersion sale at his ranch that Fall.

Now he was being forced to stand and watch his entire dream, his life's work and effort, which was totally successful as far as he was concerned, being turned over to breeders and ranchers from the entire United States. They were taking over his product that he felt only he could manage and produce. And so it went. The date of the sale arrived and with the county and his ranch swarming with millionaires, huge corporations, and large and small operators fighting and bidding and dividing up his most precious possessions, as well as A.B.'s total being. His reason for living and his sole purpose in life was all being stripped from him and he had to stand there and watch it all. The man who created and developed it all was forced to pass it on to who ever would pay the most money and he had no say about it all. No one could possibly know how much each cow, bull, or calf meant to Mr. cook personally.

But as the sale progressed he began to realize that each of those individuals were bringing such high prices and were totaling up to enough money already this far into the sale that he had more than paid the bank and all of his debts totally off.

As soon as this became clear to Mr. Cook, he climbed up on the auction podium and called an instant halt to the sale. He was now the sole owner of the remaining animals left, and he owned them totally unencumbered. The sale immediately stopped with much disagreement from the crowd of buyers who had just paid record prices for the cattle that had just been sold to them. He would honor the cattle that had sold, but there would not be one more sold here this day. And he made that statement and saw to it that that was exactly way it would be.

He stood by his word and the deeds that had been carried out against his will. He watched the last of his precious cows and herd sires leave his ranch headed for ranches clear to the east and west coast of the United States as well as many of the southern states.

But in the next few days as he inventoried the stock that was left, he realized the years, money, and effort he had experienced to build this project. A. B. Cook knew that it was totally over. He had neither the health nor the years left nor the money nor any possibility to do it all again. It was a tremendous effort and success that he could never duplicate again. As he recounted the situation, he also knew that by scattering the bloodlines far and wide and in small enough numbers as it now stood, his project was totally ended. No one would ever realize the magnitude of what he had built and to what extent it might have reached. True, his work and the breeding only he could do added a lot to the large numbers of herds who had obtained some of his cattle, but it would only go so far without his being able to enhance them for a long period of time. Basically, it became washed out in the poorer quality of those herds that did not have the continued use of his progression. It was truly the end of a huge success story at the will of a few who had the power in their hands to stop the funding, but not the foresight to watch and see what they had helped to build. The power of the few dollars they had provided became more important to them than the amazing results of how the money was being used.

In just a few short years Mr. Cook's health and drive drained out of a seriously hurt body. The real impact of all he had lost dragged him down and wasted the enthusiasm that had failed his well-being and his life long project. He was at last laid to rest on his ranch.

His son and daughter inherited the ranch but could not get along very well. His daughter too, finally broke down and passed away. His only son lived there a few more years and at least tried to maintain the ranch that had been their family home. He was not a rancher by any sense of the word. He was murdered on the ranch by a couple of young outlaws who came there one day apparently to rob him.

The ranch finally became a part of the Wellington D. Rankin estate among his vast holdings.

Mr. Cook has gone; his heirs have gone. The entire ranch and cowherd have gone, but his story is still living and is an inspiration to some who think as he did.

BROOKLIN AND
THE OLD MULE

mong my bag of tricks from out of the past, I spent a lot of my time and effort buying, selling, and trading horses as part of my means of making a living. Back in the earlier days, there weren't many phones around, and often times I would get a lead on a horse or horses for sale by word of mouth. People would tell the storekeeper, the post office clerk, or even the bartender to have me come by as they had something to sell.

On one occasion, the 71 Ranch sent word to me to stop by on such and such a day. They would have a number of horses gathered on that day, wanting to sell them and get them gone. I was very excited and grateful that they called me, because I knew some pretty nice horses would be included in the number.

The 71 Ranch was the headquarters for a very large outfit that also included six or seven other big ranches. They ran cattle numbering in the thousands and had more than several hundred horses, including a bunch of wild brood mares, from which they raised a lot of their own ranch horses.

The latest owner had passed away and his widow was in the process of shaping up the entire ranch conglomerate. She appeared to be a much better manager than her late husband had been. She surrounded herself with some very competent associates, started to clean house, and improve the entire operation.

On the designated day, I arrived at the 71 Ranch head-quarters to see about the horses they were selling. One of the new foremen met me at the corrals and explained to me that he had almost fifty head of horses. He said, "I will walk you through them, tell you the exact story on each horse, and what we expect to get for them. You can tell me what you can do, but you must buy them all as we want them gone."

We spent a couple of hours sorting and examining young colts, old ranch horses, a few unbroken horses of various descriptions, some total cripples, old mares, and a few totally wild canners. I did some figuring, arrived at an average price per head straight through, and made my offer for the lot. After a little dickering, the foreman said, "Okay. Have them out of here by tomorrow night."

I was thrilled to obtain that many horses in one deal, but now I was faced with the problem of coming up with that much money all at once, and where I'd go with all the horses. We had a ranch with good pastures and pens, but the idea would be to not feed a lot of them long enough to eat up any profits which might be had in them. I took care of the worries with the help of a friend or two and the local bank. I started hauling the horses away that evening and all the next day to get them over to our ranch.

It was really interesting and fun for me in those days—remembering cutting them into bunches according to what the foreman had told me about each one. A little Appaloosa gelding, only 12-years-old, had one eye. The foreman had said that he probably was actually the best horse on the entire ranch, but the guys working there just rode him plumb to death, and that's why they were selling him. They really wanted to see him find a good home. He was absolutely right about him; and he did find a good home. The people who wound up buying him from us used him to run their small ranch until he got too old, they then retired him, and he lived there until he died. They always said he was the best horse they had ever owned.

There were quite a number of two- and three-year-old colts that their cowboys had started and rode anywhere from 6 months to a year. They were real nice and worked out good for a number of ranches. The same was true of a few older ranch geldings that went to small ranchers who wouldn't work them too hard, and they got distributed over a pretty good-sized part of the country.

We kept some colts and broke them out to sell by the fall of next year, and so it went; older mares and a few rejects were sold to the canners. In sorting out this group, we ran into an old buckskin gelding that was 19 years old and quite plain by conformation standards. He had a large head, big feet, was real heavy boned, and was showing his age. There were a lot of saddle marks on him; he stayed off to the outside of what ever group you put him with, always by himself. Through little beady, hard, black eyes, he stood back and watched everything from as far away as he could stay. He didn't look like he trusted anybody. We had put him in several pens trying to decide which direction to go with him.

The foreman's story on him went like this. "All I know about that old buckskin horse is that Old Brooklin used to ride him all the time. He did a lot of riding on him, but I can't tell you if he's any good or if he aint. As far as I know, Brooklin is the only guy who ever got on him. That's him over there. Did you ever know Old Brooklin?"

That's where this story really begins.

Along in the early '50s, a man named Wellington D. Rankin, a very shrewd and powerful attorney, started buying up ranches around the towns of Martinsdale, White Sulphur Springs, and Ringling County of Montana. Before he was done, he had put together a very large ranch stretching from the Canadian Border to the Wyoming line, and reaching both east and west throughout a good portion of the length of Montana. He bought land that consisted of some of the best ranch country available in the world. Because of the scope of countryside he had put together, his ranches included flat gumbo country, high and steep mountains, nice river valleys, cliff and badland type country, and large sagebrush flats. He had hay farmland and extremely good grass pasture land.

In some cases, he had sold enough timber off parts of the ranches he'd bought to pay for them and others included. He was very shrewd, but his management techniques were anything but shrewd. In fact, he didn't manage at all. He would get prisoners, out on work release from the local penitentiaries, to work on the ranches. This could have been all right, had he got some good help. It seemed that most of the people he got didn't know much about ranching and wouldn't work at all.

He had a commissary on the 71 Ranch and kept many of these prisoners there. When they came, they were made to sign a contract and were not allowed to leave the ranch.

He would usually end up sending them back to their prisons before their contracts were up, so he didn't have to pay them. There was always a few that had the feeling they got cheated, feeling very badly toward him, and often times tried to get something for their money's worth. Sometime they would sell things from his commissary, or steal calves, or do whatever they could do to rectify their feelings of being cheated, never doing much of anything constructive for the good of his ranch.

One day, after this had gone on for a few years, there was a little feller that showed up out in one of the line camps. He called himself, Brooklin. He had a very heavy eastern accent and possessed the mannerisms of someone definitely not from our part of the country. I, myself, do not know how or when Brooklin showed up, but from whatever day it was, he stayed on the Rankin Ranch and worked there the rest of his life. I knew of him being around for at least fifteen years and always stayed out in some outlying line camp, but would go to all of the Rankin owned ranches to gather and work cattle. He got to know all of the pastures and different ranches and became accepted as pretty good help. Everyone who worked with him realized he was a good guy, and became his friend. He never did look like he belonged out there in that rough and tough country, but he never quit, and he always pulled his weight one way or another. They all had many stories about him and laughed a lot—not at him, but with him.

I stopped at his line camp on a very cold winter day. Brooklin was out trying to break some ice in a water trough. He had tied a large towel around his neck and made a sling for one of his arms. While riding, he said his horse had fell and, as a result, he broke his collarbone. He was out there all alone, living in a tiny little cabin not a lot better than an old bunkhouse. I'll never know how he kept from freezing to death. Whenever they needed him to be at one of the other ranches, they would send someone for him and his old buckskin gelding, haul them over, and had them stay and work until they got through. Then they'd put him back out all alone in some other camp. He never ever had any clothes or equipment. Everything he owned, someone either gave him, or another worker had left it behind; once it was in his sight, he used what ever it might be.

He had shown up for work wearing gloves and shoes that were not mates. Sometimes, he wore a huge woolen overcoat like someone well dressed might wear to a funeral. Once, for about a week in cold weather, he wore an old army uniform someone said he found in an abandoned cabin. He had nothing—certainly no money. Every once in awhile, some of the neighbors who ran across him would give him a coat or some warm clothes, hoping to keep him from freezing to death. He never asked anyone for anything, but he never turned down a handout.

He often told stories of his experiences and what he had seen. Everyone who heard his stories would debate for days whether or not they believed them to be true. I don't know that anybody ever knew for sure where he had come from, how he ever had ended up here, or what he had done in his life. Brooklin was the only name anyone ever knew to call him and even his age was debatable. Most people believed him to be much older than they would think. The only thing everyone agreed on was that he wasn't getting any younger.

One thing that Brooklin was consistent about was his buckskin gelding. It is assumed that when he came to work on the Rankin Ranch, the gelding was one of the horses there. Brooklin at once claimed the gelding as his personal horse and kept him from then on. He always rode him every day for every job, whether that job lasted two hours or two months. Nobody ever saw the old horse give him any trouble, but Brooklin would quite often tell his closest friends that the buckskin had bucked him off yesterday, or last week, or that he expected him to buck today. Many times he would show up walking lame, or all skinned up, and swear old Buck had bucked him off again. But no one ever saw it happen, and they used to make jokes with him about his big stories. He would never get offended and would stick to his story.

A few months before I got to buy this bunch of horses, someone had found Brooklin out in one of those line camps. He had died out in the yard. They figured it was either from a heart attack or a stroke. He had died alone, and it happened long before he was found. No one could tell if he died quickly or maybe had lain out for a time.

It was of very little concern to most people, but the small group of ranchers and cowboys, who had had the privilege of working with him, and knowing him, knew they would really miss him. They all felt he had contributed something special to them, and that the story of his life was very lonely and sad. I would even wonder if, to this day, there would be anyone who could point out the location of his grave.

A few days after I had got this bunch of horses home, I was deciding the fate of each one; I received word from a good friend by the name of Irvin Cooper. Cooper had always been one of Brooklin's best friends and had worked with him probably as much as anybody. Inquiring, he wanted to know if I had got the old buckskin gelding that Brooklin always rode and, if so, would I sell him. I finally got hold of Cooper and told him "yes" to both questions—I had the buckskin, and I would sell him. It really took a load off my mind that someone like Cooper would have a need for the old buckskin, because I sure didn't want to see him canned, but I couldn't see any other use for him.

Eventually, we agreed on $300 as a fair price. When Cooper had loaded him up and was ready to leave our place with him, he said, "Old Brooklin used to always claim that this horse would buck him off, and I always figured maybe he could buck if he had a chance. I would like to see if he might be pretty good. We shook hands good-bye, and, in a cloud of dust, Cooper and the Brooklin Buckskin headed down the road to a brand new career at nineteen years of age.

Before long, Irvin had got some pretty tough boys to try the Buckskin out and, after the first couple of tries, found out that he couldn't find a cowboy who could ride him. He had decided to try bucking him bareback to make it a little easier on him, and he bucked one after another off, including one of the leading contenders from the PRCA National Finals Cowboys. In a little while, Dale Small, a leading rodeo contractor in the Montana area, leased the Buckskin and renamed him The Old

Mule. Soon, his large posters read, "Another Dale Small Rodeo featuring The Old Mule." They said the horse was a natural and really enjoyed the life of a professional bareback bucking bronc. Hundreds of people flocked to the rodeos where he participated to see if this time he would be ridden or not.

As late as the time the horse had turned twenty-three-years-old, he had not yet been ridden. He was nominated for, and performed at, the National Finals in Oklahoma City a couple of times. He built and enhanced his career for another few years. Finally, Dale Small sold his rodeo string. But The Old Mule kept bucking, and became better known than all of the people in his life. Some said he did it for Brooklin and in his later years, he brought a little fame to them both.

It would be nice to believe that by now, maybe he and Brooklin are sitting out on some high vantage point on an unending nice, warm, sunny day, overlooking the thousands of acres they once worked and cared for together. The place we remember as the old 71 Ranch.

POPEYE

long in the early 1990s we had established a herd
of 30 brood mares and ranching was at that time,
one of the leading industries working pretty well in
all of the western states from Arizona to Montana, Texas,
Idaho, California, and New Mexico. Our effort at that time
was to help stock a few of those ranches with cow horses
and occasionally, a few were working out pretty good as
rodeo rope horses. Mexico was also one of our best outlets.

All of our bloodlines were working stock horses and all of our efforts went into making good ranch horses. We were trying to place our horses along these lines while buying quite a few outside horses that we would sell to these same buyers. At that time we broke our own colts. Between riding our young ones and buying and selling what we could gather up required quite a lot of traveling. We kept very busy and managed to create a pretty decent reputation of which we were very proud. We worked hard at honoring that and protecting our good name as that seemed to be the key to building a bigger business based almost entirely on repeat customers.

Each fall we started all of our now just past 2-year-olds and rode them thru the winter, and by spring the customers would be looking for some new horses.

Among our band of brood mares, we had bought an older My Texas Dandy and Cutter Bill bred mare, which had been raised by the University of Arizona. We were crossing her on a Boston Mac bred stallion we owned for about 8 years called Bostons Tea Party.

The cross between him and this My Texas Dandy mare had produced a number of exceptionally good looking and quite growthy foals, which seemed to catch the eyes of a lot of people. They would usually sell before we ever got a chance to ride them. But I believe along about '94, the mare had produced a little black colt that for some reason didn't get very big. He was tremendously built but just not very tall. By the Fall of his 2-year-old year, he was still living here with us, and we didn't get him started because he seemed to be too small. Through his growing up years and halter breaking, trimming his feet, and all that we had done with him, we still had a little horse that was pretty scared of us but who would not run away when we went to catch him. Instead of running away, he would just stand and quiver all over, crouch down real low, and then his big black eyes would just bug way out of his head. Therefore, we named him "Popeye." It was a name that stuck and he wore it for the rest of his life.

You could walk up to him in a whole herd of horses and he'd turn to face you, crouch down, shiver, and just stand his ground. You could touch him and pet him and even halter him while his eyes were popping way out of his head. He would lead right off and was very pleasant to handle but catching him got to be a real fun experience.

We kept Popeye well into his 3-year-old year and had started riding a new bunch of two year olds when one day I decided it was time to start little Popeye. So off he went to the training barn with a half dozen or so of his little 2-year-old brothers who were all ready quite a lot bigger than him.

He seemed to start quite easy, never bucked and wasn't bronky. Within a couple of days, I climbed on and began riding him. I was pretty impressed with Popeye. About the third time I had ridden him he was starting, stopping, turning around pretty good, and I thought I would head outside on him as he sure was doing good. But I noticed my blanket had slid back a little, so I thought I better straighten it up. Stepping off of him, I loosened the cinch enough to slide the blanket forward without unsaddling him completely. The second I did this the ball opened. He spun around, jerked away from me, and tore down the full length of about 100 yards of alley, which is where I'd been riding him. When he got to the end of the alley, he didn't even consider slowing down but just plowed head first into the fence and sent oil field pipe and sucker rod flying in every direction. He bored a hole the exact size of himself through that fence and wound up outside that alley and into a big pen several hundred feet square. By this time my saddle had turned under his belly and pieces of my saddle were flying off and scattered everywhere marking the trail he had made going all the way around that pen. He ended up stopping beside the water trough about in the middle of the fence along the north side. His eyes were very big and bugging way outside his face, and his little sides were pumping heavily from all the effort he had exerted, as it had been an extremely fast trip.

I eased up on him checking for injuries and being careful not to set him off again. As I retrieved my saddle from him, a little stream of blood started seeping from under his foretop from a 2-inch cut along the top of his head right between his ears. I couldn't see any other damage except for the fence and my saddle, which were both extremely in need of a lot of repair. But one thing I did notice was that Popeye was no longer content to stand close to me and shake or shiver, instead he was trying to leave. It seemed that he had decided he didn't want to ever see that saddle again and the far end of his lead rope or my bridle reins were absolutely as close as he and I were ever going to be again.

After awhile, I decided to put him back in his stall and let him digest all that had gone on. I wanted to be sure that he wasn't hurt someplace I couldn't see like a neck injury or blindness. I got him to his stall in the barn and tried to pet him and console him. I finally got his halter off and turned him loose. For three days I fed him and tried to touch him and calm him down but to no avail. Popeye had turned very wild. He wouldn't turn his head toward me, and I didn't think it looked like a very good idea to try to touch his rear end. I believed I would wear his footprints for the rest of my life. So after another day or two, I worked him out into an outside pen and turned him completely loose. I was sick about it all and figured I had done him about as much damage as I could ever hope to have done. But I sure had plenty more to do and before long a month had gone by.

One evening, just as darkness was falling, a vehicle drove into our yard and a young man got out and said he was from Albuquerque, New Mexico. He had stopped by to see if we had any unbroke colts to sell. As we walked through a few and visited a little, he spotted Popeye standing off by himself out there and he said, " My golly, what's the story on that horse?" I told him the whole story and he interrupted me before I could finish saying, "What would you take for him? I like him." We agreed on a price and he said, "I will write you a check now and pick him up in just 2 days." And it was done. Popeye's and my adventures had just come to an end.

The kid did exactly as he said he would do, and every time I tried to explain to him why Popeye was a little distant, he would only say, "He is just exactly what I wanted."

I was a little bit relieved to think Popeye was leaving, but I had really grown attached to him and hated to see him leave, hating me so badly and feeling so mixed up, as he sure had seemed to have such a good side. We brought him into the pens with a few of his little pals and eventually loaded him on the boy's stock trailer. I was sure glad to see that he hadn't come with a 2-horse trailer as so often happens.

After the boy and Popeye drove away, I didn't hear anything from either one of them for about a month, so one day I called him on a number he had left with me. We had a little conversation and, finally, I asked him how he and Popeye were getting along and he said, "Oh, good." I asked if he was riding him yet, and he said, "No, not yet, but I think I will be in about a month."

About 2 years went by and although Popeye crossed my mind every so often, I was almost afraid to call the kid again to inquire about our little black horse when a stranger stopped at our place on some business. He ended up saying, " By the way, I saw a black horse of yours in a rodeo a month or so ago, he had your keyhole brand on him and they said his name was Popeye. Man, did he ever buck." I asked, "Did the cowboy ride him?" and he said, "Oh hell, no! He barely got out of the chute!" I didn't know if that was a good story or a very sad one.

For a few years, every once in awhile, someone would mention they had seen Popeye perform in a rodeo somewhere. It seemed a lot of people became aware of the little black horse with the keyhole brand on his right thigh named Popeye.

Several more years went by and the stories seemed to cease. At last my memories of Popeye sort of wasted away as there were many more horses that came and went and each left a story in my memory.

There was even a day Bostons Tea Party and the little brown My Texas Dandy mare each left us and our operation in lieu of other mares and stallions. Times changed and ranching began to give way to tourists and developers. The entire horse business changed and it became harder to recall and keep track of a lot of the important past experiences and occurrences.

There was an old rancher named Joe and his son Charlie who were amazing hold outs in this area of Arizona where we live. They bought out many neighbors' old ranches and are now considered very large and very successful. Charlie, like his father, is widely admired and recognized as a tough and successful rancher. His father had become a legend and was nearing the end of his life, but through the consistent efforts of Charlie, they continued to forge on daily.

One day about a year ago a ranch hand from their ranch came to our place and while visiting and told me about his adventures there. He said, "Do you happen to remember a little black horse? He's got your brand on him, and they call him Popeye. That rancher bought him from some guy a couple of years ago and he is his very favorite horse. Evidently, his rodeo career was relatively short lived. Although he was definitely considered a cowboy's horse, Charlie was evidently the one who came along in Popeye's life to help him on the road to become his favorite ranch horse after having experienced his other avenues. No one else ever touches him. But anytime they really have a tough job to do that old boy rides Popeye. He doesn't ever let anyone else touch him. Man, he's a good horse!" To me that story touched me more than almost

91

anything I could of ever heard. I just have to believe there could only be one of them horses and I can get a lot of mileage out of retracing his footsteps even though Popeye did it all without me. It is a very interesting success story for him to be that rancher's favorite horse. I believe he is also mine.

A LADY AND
HER MULE

he phone rang and rang again. It was the end of
a very normal day and everything seemed to be
winding down, until the interruption of the phone
ringing three times. As I picked up the receiver to answer
it, I had no idea where the call would lead.

A lady's voice sounded a little bit shy on the other end,

as she inquired as to whether she had reached the horse sale place. I assured her, "Yes, you have. Can I help you?" But from there on it was strictly her one-way conversation. She inquired about when our next sale was, how were horses selling lately, and how many were we expecting at the next sale? Before I could answer those questions, she continued to ask if we ever get any mules in the sale. I just cut all my answers short and said, "Oh, yeah, quite often. Are you looking for a mule?" Her answer was another question, "Oh, no. What do they usually bring?" But again my attempt to answer was cut short with more questions from her. More questions followed before I could come up with an answer for one or two of the first questions. Again, I managed to ask, "If you're not looking for a mule maybe you have one you're thinking of selling?" The questions pretty much stopped and everything got much quieter as she finally said, "I haven't really decided yet, but I'll let you know." It sounded like she might be going to hang up, so I said, "Could I get your name or number and I'll call you back a little closer to sale day?" She just answered, "Oh, no, that's okay. I'll just call back," and she hung up.

I worried that I had somehow really offended her. I thought maybe her questions had kept coming so fast and my cutting the answers so short trying to keep up, she might have thought, "Hey, that guy sure don't know much or maybe just wouldn't answer all my questions." But whatever she thought, she left me with no option of ever calling her back or giving her any more information.

I decided that maybe she couldn't think of anything good to say about her mule, or maybe she couldn't decide whether she really wanted to sell him at a sale. (*and have to be responsible for what the mule might do to the buyer.*) The only thing that I could see plainly was that I was not going to get any more information about the mule. I took the whole phone call to mean she was likely not a real good woman to sell a mule to, or anything else for that matter. That was about as far as I though about phone call for about the next week and a half.

About three days before the next sale, I came into the house around dark and there was a call on the answering machine. The message said, "This is the lady you talked to the other night inquiring about selling my mule. I have decided to bring him to your sale."

In the message there was no mention about age, disposition, color, and still no phone number to call and get more information. The message only said that she would bring him to the sale. A quality mule is good to have as a consignment in a sale. We try hard to pass along the information on all the incoming consignments because that's the only way we can do our best to get them sold. Once in a while all those stories about how good the mule is, don't turn out to be true; quite often they are more the consignor's opinion than anyone else's. In this case I was thinking this one could be disastrous, and quite possibly we wouldn't see her at all.

The last couple of days before a sale go by very fast and the first thing I know, it is sale day and things are very busy. The sale was progressing right along with all of the tack getting sold, and then the horses were being brought into the sale barn to begin the auction. We had shown four or five horses when I realized we had not seen any mules. It's necessary to keep the auction moving quite fast, as that is what people expect to see happen. You try to determine fair prices, encourage a little good will from the audience, and add some fever into the bidding. It's important to have the people who are bringing in their horses to sell, feel that you are trying your best for them. A big legitimate nice gelding had just sold, after we had taken a little extra time to with his sale to make sure we brought in the highest price. That's when I noticed a very nice truck and trailer pull up to the front door of the sale ring. As the big gelding was exiting the sale ring and the next horse was about to enter, I watched the driver of the truck walk out to the back end of the trailer and stand by the end gate. Eventually I saw a lady appear and walk the full length of the truck–she was very nicely dressed and you couldn't help notice she was tremendously crippled. In fact, she was walking with the help of hand crutches upon her arriving at the end gate. I could see a very gorgeous little black mule with tall white stockings unload from the trailer. They both disappeared from my sight and into a pen as I was forced to turn my attention back to selling the next horse, which had now entered the sale ring. The sale racked up some good sales and some not so good with both happy and not so happy consignors carrying on their business.

After another dozen or so horses came through the sale, the in gate swung open and the little black mule was led into the ring by the man I had seen drive up. I knew that I had not seen the mule before and with the fast way that he got into the sale ring in the short time it had been since he arrived at the sale, the management people recognized very good potential in him and had salvaged a speedy number to get him into the sale.

The man led the little mule up in front of the crowd and after a very short moment turned toward the gate and motioned to someone to come toward him, but we could hear a woman's voice saying, " No. I can't do that." The man very calmly just said, "Yes, you can. Come in and tell them your story and show these people what he does." The same crippled lady I had seen earlier, unloading the mule continued with a little more protesting as she hobbled into the ring. The mule turned very carefully to meet her. Very patiently and with kindness in his voice man quietly said to the lady, "Get on him and show your mule to these people."

She said, "No!" again and again. "I cannot do this," but the man handed her the bridle reins and stepped off out of the way. There was a deafening silence in the sale ring-every eye in the crowd was focused on the lady and her mule. Everyone watched as the mule faced the lady squarely and then slowly sank down right on his belly, as she very awkwardly stepped up and climbed onto his back. Once she was securely mounted and ready, he, like a little hydraulic machine, slowly and without so much as a jump or a jerk rose up and stood tall on his 4 feet. The man, who was the lady's husband, said softly, "Now tell them your story."

Three things took place all at once as this lady, showing more strength and courage then you could ever imagine, started speaking. First, the lady said in a strong voice, "I raised this little mule from a baby-I've had him all his life. I broke him and have ridden him all over the country, the

COWBOY STORIES: GRIT, HORSES, AND FAITH

Grand Canyon, many nationally known pleasure rides all over the west, and he has taken the very best care of me and given me all of the pleasures that I could have ever asked for. But as you see now, I can no longer go and do those things, but he still can and will for someone else here today. I cannot bear to see him stand and wait for me any longer. He wants to go and do things. That is why I am selling him today." As she spoke, she guided him around in that crowd of people, and he rode strictly all business for anything she asked.

The second thing that happened was that I suddenly realized why the lady on the phone could not tell me whether or not she was going to sell her mule. It was most certainly evident that she had spent weeks, days, and hours making up her mind whether or not to sell him. I knew then she must have rehearsed many times the scene where she would walk into his pen and say her last good bye to this great little friend of hers and then have to turn to walk away and not look back, not really knowing who would be taking him to his new home. I cannot fathom how much courage it took for her to do this. It must have also occurred to her that after all they had been through together, this little ride in the sale ring would be their very last and she was taking her very last ride on him and probably forever.

The third thing that took place in that crowd of several hundred people who had heard the lady speak, was that there not one dry eye. Even the auctioneer was affected, and could not start his bid calling. There were no tears however, in the eyes of that brave and strong lady. She was doing what she figured she had to do, facing the future and her badly deteriorating health.

No matter what the mule sold for, as I watched him sold and walking out of the ring I was sure that in no way was it what he was really worth. The lady took the sale price, and most graciously thanked everyone for their help.

I did not witness her leaving the sale but when it was over she and her husband were gone. The mule and his new owner had also gone, and to this day I know not what became of them all.

What is left of the lady and her mule is the way they looked that day of their last ride together in the auction barn. I will never forget the humility, grace the lady left with me that day, in her selfless decision to sell that mule.

ALL IS NOT GOLD THAT GLITTERS

Throughout the years I've found that in a lot of ways life is like one big horse trade. Many things that you run across in daily occurrences are like sitting at a horse sale evaluating each horse that enters the ring as a potential opportunity or possible bonanza and even realizing it might be a bad idea all together-but that one alone you try stay away from. The first two examples are usually why you become involved. Oftentimes looking back you wonder what you missed that was so obvious just a couple of days later.

My wife, who I always felt was a very good judge of horseflesh, did quite a bit of buying and selling very successfully for years. But she, too, had her success stories as well as failures.

One day right here at our horse sale we had a pretty heavy run of all classes of horses. The sale was nearing the end when a man from up in the Safford area came into the ring with a pretty black 4-year-old colt. He appeared really nice and sure sported a pretty build with his actions and conformations.

My wife watched them in the ring for a few minutes as the bidding slowly started and I soon saw her getting into the bidding-a few passes back and forth and she was the high bidder at $450.00. She was quite happy.

Later on into the day she explained to me how she had noticed the colt when he came to the sale and went out to the arena to watch him ride. But she said she was a little bit confused as she noticed that the rider didn't seem to want to lope him. He told her all about the colt and answered most of her questions, but each time she said, "Will he lope?" The guy would say, "Oh, sure," but then would walk him off out of hearing distance and never make the horse go into any other gait, just walk.

Sunday morning she was right out there ready to ride her new colt she had bought the day before. She saddled him up with no problems, but felt she could detect a little hump there in his back so she jipped him around the arena a little. She then repeated her story to me about what she had witnessed the day before. Handing me the bridle reins she asked me if I would ride him. Of course I had only one answer and that was after I cleared my throat a time or two. I said, "Well, sure." So I stepped on him right there in the arena. I, too, noticed the hump in his back, but I also found that after he walked off about 30 steps it seemed to disappear and he went around pretty nice. He obviously traveled out quite nice and soon he broke into a nice little slow lope. He stopped and turned around appearing to ride okay. Probably after about a half an hour of my riding on him I gave him back to her and just before she could get time to get on him, a customer came to pay and do some business. By the time he left she had other things to attend to so she put him away. She had now owned him about 36 hours.

COWBOY STORIES: GRIT, HORSES, AND FAITH

The next day, Monday morning, was busy for a little while and as soon as it slowed down a little she saddled up her colt again and lead him over to the arena. As he stepped through the gate into the arena he jerked away from her and bucked about 3 times around the arena harder than I had seen a horse buck in a long time. That was not a good sign. Our thoughts immediately went to a young cowboy who had been plaguing us for a job for several weeks; he claimed he was a bronc rider.

So we finally got a hold of him and he was thrilled. "Yes, sir, I would be happy to try him for you. We'll get him straightened right out." I knew he wouldn't have to pay any attention to me as I was glad to say I had taken my turn on him Sunday morning.

By about 12 noon the young cowboy whose name was Clint arrived and saddled up the colt and stepped up on him. He rode him around for about fifteen minutes and said, "Let me out of here. I'm going to go out and show this colt some country." Which was exactly what you would have thought ought to be done except for one thing. Just about 100 yards outside of the arena the colt blew up again and in about 4 jumps had really unloaded Clint, jerked away from him, and came loping right back to the arena. We corralled him, got Clint reoriented, and he went back to the arena to try him again. "This time," said Clint, "I will ride a little more and get a sweat up on him in this long alley." Which again I thought would be the thing to do. But as Clint stepped up on him, the little black colt buried his head, bucked Clint off in about 2 jumps, and ran away from him to the far end of the alley. Clint was up pretty quick that time and catching him up again ended up with his head drove into the ground in seconds coming back down the alley. "This time," he said, "I guess we better take him to the round pen and spend a little more time on him." And this we did except upon entering the round pen, the colt busted into again and bucking blindly across the round pen hit the fence and wound up reaching out under the wall with a front foot and completely tore his hoof wall off of his front foot.

He came running back across the round pen towards us waving a badly injured and bleeding foot at us and very bewilderedly just stood holding his foot up off the ground.

Clint was apologizing over and over and all I could say was, "I don't see where it was any of your fault. If anything, it was our fence that injured him, but I think we have gone out and bought a very counterfeit little horse here."

Just at that very moment, a truck drove into our yard and it was Doc Arters our veterinarian. He walked up to us and saw in an instant what was happening. We asked Doc what can we possibly do now with this deal? Doc said, "Well, if you want my advice, by the time you doctor him for about $2000 and wait for about 2 more years for that foot to grow out then he'll be 7 or 8 years old and you can start breaking him over again. My advice is to euthanize him right now.

Once again that day I had to say it looks like just what a man ought to do and so we did.

Lisa had by now still only owned him about 40 hours.

I always had to take my hat off to the consignor who had brought him in as he somehow along the way put a good start of a handle on him and quite obviously probably with the aid of a snubbing horse put some miles on him.

He just didn't bother to explain a few things about his habits to the lady who thought he looked pretty nice that day at the horse sale in Benson.

In less than two days her plans for him and her hopes of any profits along with her purchase price were lost forever and her ideas for the gold had turned into dust. It happens every once in awhile.

BEANO LYONS AND OLD PAINT

From the time I can first remember Beano, he had already lived a pretty long and active life. He had been born to affluent parents and had become a very well known rancher. His parents had been named among the oldest settlers in the Mussellshell Valley and especially in the location known as Two Dot country.

They started their ranch, which was named the "GL Ranch" after their brand, and the name was still very common even during my grown-up years. It was still well known after having been handed through his parents, his generation, his kids' generation, and on into his grandson's time, who was close to my age. His grandson, Jim, and I were at least as close as brothers and spent many experiences together resulting in a lifelong friendship, which, as far as I'm concerned, still exists to this day.

Though time and miles have now sorted us apart for many years, he is still one of the people I think of very often. His father and he each inherited the same nickname as Jim's grandfather, Beano. Long before I was old enough to hear any of the stories that were most affectionately told over and over and from far and wide about old Beano Lyons, I had met him. In spite of the accomplishments, amusing stories, sadness and happiness that revolved around his life, my most favorites have always been my first memories of him.

As far as I can recollect, I was probably about four or five years old when I remember on cold Montana winter days, while outside playing around the ranch, I'd spot Beano coming toward our place. At that time, he was always on horseback. He was running a trap line, trapping beaver, muskrat, bobcats, and, occasionally, a coyote or some other fur-bearing animal unlucky enough to get caught in his traps.

Approaching our place from the route of his trap line, he would appear on a little hill just to the west of our line fence, which bordered the ranch his son ran for Beano's wife's family and his sister-in-law. I used to spot him coming and run to the gate to meet him and open it for him. I feel now, and felt very much back then, that Beano Lyons was a friend of mine. I don't really know how old he was then, but he seemed old to me. I suppose maybe he was in his sixties, which I considered old, up until just a few years ago when I myself reached that age.

I will never forget his same greeting to me each time as I would open the gate to let him in. I would say, "Hi Beano," and he would always answer back, "How's us kids today?" While sitting on his horse, he'd start telling me stories as I shut the gate. I'd walk along beside him, hanging on his every word, as he picked his way on out through our yard and corral area. He wanted to get over along side the river so he could continue on his trap line. Usually, he would have a beaver or muskrat tied on to his saddle, which he would proudly show me, and I was always anxious to look at.

Once in awhile, he would tie up his horse and come up to the house to warm up a little. Whether he stopped or not, he would always inquire about the health and wellbeing of my parents and our family. Occasionally, he brought with him news from the community as to how the war was going, who might be sick, who had passed away, or just any items of interest. He was always tuned in to the affairs of everyone, as he was definitely a friend to them all.

In spite of the time that has passed, I can still see him riding from the farthest distance away, as he rode up close, he sat on a horse like a man who had spent many hours there. He had grown a little stocky and was never a very tall man, but his old legs and body had definitely obtained the shape of a man molded to his horse. He rode an old

A Fork saddle which, I suppose, he had owned since he was a young man just starting out, as it was old, but still serviceable. He always wore wool pants, a wool shirt, and a wool coat, which I can't ever remember seeing buttoned up. His face was quite large, nearly round, and looked exactly like the frozen country he would ride in every day. Deeply lined, weathered, and set in a very still, but pleasant expression.

The other thing about Beano, maybe even more memorable than he himself, was his horse. He was fairly small, but a real stocky sorrel and white paint gelding, he called, "Paint." If there was anyone in the country as well known and appreciated maybe more than Beano, it was sure enough Paint. He looked exactly like just what he was; an old ranch-type horse, a trapper's horse, and, certainly, a relic of times past. Again, I don't know how old Paint was either, but I do know he had been around a long time and was around during my growing up years. If my memories are straight, I believe he outlived Beano himself, as I remember him retired and running with all of the teams and ranch horses on the Freezer ranch for many years.

Maybe it was because I was young, or because I was interested in animals, history, cowboys, and ranch people, but to this day, I can still feel the same excitement that I felt as a child when I looked out across the snow covered hills and watched as Beano and Paint as they would appear on the skyline. Often the wind would be so bad, that it would make your eyes water, and you'd have to shut your eyes, and hold your hands over your face to keep watching him as he approached. He was a figure from the past with an extremely exciting history, which even at that time, I realized that one day I would never see again. I learned later to look for the same profile in every one of Charlie Russell's paintings. I've seen many attempts to duplicate that profile over the years in the good old western movies. I have heard many stories told about Beano Lyons, and some of his old friends, which will always remain imbedded in my imagination and I'll always remember his actions I used to see whenever he'd arrive. He and his mannerisms were so genuine. He was a perfect example of the old saying, "The salt of the earth." I looked for and enjoyed seeing him for few more years until one day, I realized it was not happening anymore.

I guess, at first, Beano quit trapping and, eventually, just became a little more attached to his home. As I got older, I would see him once in awhile on the streets of Two Dot. Then, like many of his friends and neighbors, each in their own experience, they just passed on; their stories and memories lingered a little while longer, and then you realize times have changed.

It is the way.

BEANO EPILOGUE

During the years I went to school in Two Dot, which was pretty close to a half mile out on the east edge of town, almost all of us kids used to watch from the school windows, the herds of sheep and cattle as they were trailed in from summer pastures. In the fall of the year, we would watch as they were being headed back out to winter on many of the ranches out south of Two Dot. Often times, those same ranchers would bring their stock to town to be shipped back east. We would race over to the windows each time to stand and watch them go through town, as we all knew whose they were. We recognized the horses and pack mules from each ranch. We knew them all by name and most of the old ranch hands that would be helping to drive them. Although most hands would have changed the ranches they worked for during the year, you could be sure the saddle horses, packhorses, and mules could always tell who belonged to whom. That is still one of my most favorite recollections.

That, too, just one day ceased to happen.

FRANK ROBERTSON

rank Robertson was born back in Astoria, Illinois, in May of 1866. The Civil War was just over and that war had a lot of people, both north and south of the Mason-Dixon Line, left wondering which side they really agreed with. It caused a lot of hard feelings in many families and between neighbors. But most everyone was trying to patch things up and get back on a steady keel as

Peace had been declared and there was, like always, new problems to deal with.

Frank's family had participated to a large degree in that war and, as he grew up, there was always kind of an urge to get away, to go some place else, and get involved in some of the country's other problems.

There was always that country out west calling and most all young men were attracted to the opportunities and adventures they knew lay out beyond the Mississippi, and all they had heard about Montana and the land beyond the Missouri River, which was accessible by steamboat at that time.

Frank came from a long line of livestock people and, especially, horsemen. He had older brothers and grandparents who traded horses, worked teams, and were good teachers for him. He definitely found a lot of interest in horses and was becoming quite an accomplished horseman in his own right. The boys, in those days, grew up early and accepted responsibility at a pretty young age. Frank must have been only around 16-years-old when he decided to go west and become a cowpuncher.

He soon found himself out west and wound up as far as Sprague, Washington. Over the next four years, about the time he was just 20-years-old, he was heading back into North Dakota. He was trailing on horseback a herd of horses, which he successfully delivered to some men named Walford and Masterson around Lisbon, North Dakota. He had made the trip, in part, on his way back to Astoria to marry his boyhood sweetheart, a gal named Luta McClelland, which he pulled off successfully. While enroute back to Washington, they ended up in Castle,

Montana, for a spell and, eventually, settled down about 40 miles further east. They remained in the Two Dot area for the rest of their lives.

During his next 40 years of life, he was mostly a cowboy and worked the big country, as there were no fences for the large herds of cattle belonging to only a few ranchers. He saw the droughts and the hard winters. He saw gold strikes and mining camps, outlaws, and the rough and tough lives of those towns that sprang up from nowhere when gold was found and then disappeared over night when most people decided lady luck wasn't all that kind to them. He saw, to a pretty good degree, the end of the Indian wars and experienced the problems that came with the fall of the Indians' original way of life. He saw the building of the railroads and early day roads. He freighted with his own teams and wagons when there were not any roads at all. He lived a little of the history of the passing of the west. He knew men like C.M. Russell, Charlie Bair, Wallis Hiedikuper, Will Rogers, Two Dot Wilson, and many famous Indians.

It is no wonder he grew up to be the man he did. From the stories people tell about him, he was among the last of the real old breed. He had been a bronc rider, a well-known cowboy, and a veterinarian. He'd had a homestead or two, several mail contracts in his older years, and had freighted goods for all of the ranches both into and back from areas where the railroads and steamboats could get. He raised a family who stayed there for another generation after his passing, had grandkids who remained after that, and his descendents are still in the area. The stories that were repeated only make those of us who came along

113

after him wish we could have shaken his hand and had him tell us what he saw, what he did, and what he forgot.

When I was growing up, I had ladies who I considered old at the time, that were born and raised around Two Dot tell me stories. "Why, I remember your grandfather; he was so handsome and polite, so well mannered, and gracious. He had the most magnificent head of silver hair, which he'd had since he was 21 years of age." These stories were told to me 25 and 30 years after his passing. Others remembered him riding a bucking horse down the main streets of Big Elk and Two Dot while holding a bottle of whiskey in both hands during private celebrations and general get-togethers.

Several people remembered one story that tells a little bit about his integrity and is quite amusing. In his later years, he totally quit drinking. But on one of his and Luta's anniversaries, some old friends gave them a fancy bottle of whiskey. Luta placed it on the buffet in their dining room and it sat there for a number of years as a centerpiece. Maybe it even had a little sentimental value as it came from good friends on an important anniversary. Frank and Luta had a young son born quite late in their married years; their youngest daughter being 18-years-old when he was born, and he was now around 15-years-old. John, or Buster as he was often called, and a friend of his began to eye the bottle of whiskey and thought it might be a pretty good joke to drink it. They devised a plan to drink the whiskey and replace it with tea when they knew Frank and Luta would be gone for the day.

Again, it sat there for a few months unnoticed. One day, while doing her housework, Luta discovered the switched

114

bottle of tea and immediately assumed Frank had slipped in, drank the whiskey, and tried to fool her with the tea.

Luta was well known for speaking her piece anyway and, when she did collar Frank, it was not a pretty sight. They say there was some name calling and accusing fingers pointed at him and a scorching dressing down probably far beyond what was necessary.

Young Buster was also present and heard every word that she said. He didn't know what to do, so he didn't do anything. He just listened and said that Frank did the same. He stood there and let Luta run on until she just plain couldn't say anything more and, I guess, turned and stormed away. He said Frank just took the chewing out and let it all go by. Buster said that as far as he ever found out, Frank never ever told her or mentioned it to him to his dying day.

Another time, not too far from the end of his life, he was staying at a boarding house in Harlowton in order to be a little closer to an old time hospital that was operating there.

They claim Frank walked into the boarding house dining room one night and had obviously been in a pretty bad fight. He was bruised and a little battered and was traveling pretty slow. A stranger that evening asked a few people who were watching, "What is the matter with you people here? Why would you sit around here and let an old man like that get all beat up and not one of you steps in or does anything about it?"

Some of them laughed and said, "You think he needs some one to step in and help him? You need to see the other two guys, because I don't think they've even got up yet."

He was truly one of the old guard who did his thing and didn't ask anyone for much. But it is because of his kind that the country, and the people, were better off for a while. And together, along with others of his time, they have passed on and left us a hard trail to follow, but they damn sure left a plain trail.

HARLEY'S
STEP CHILD

t has been often seen how men have been made fun of, been proven wrong, been beat, or been embarrassed because of their belief in a horse. And just as often, and on a much better note, men have been pleased, proud, and received much acclaim because of their efforts and actions and accomplishments with horses. Horses are a lot like humans; sometimes they do well, and sometimes they fail, mostly just because they are horses. They are living their individual day-to-day lives around the intentions and expectations of some human.

This is a true story about a horse and a few of the men who owned him. Most of the names and places in this story are left out in an effort to tell the story more accurately.

This October morning, Harley was up at his usual 5:00 a.m. and had barely got his coffee started when the phone rang. The minute he answered it, he knew there was something pretty unusual about to happen when the voice on the other end said pleasantly, "Good morning Harley, have you got the coffee pot on yet?" It was the familiar voice of one of his closest friends, John. They only lived like about 12 miles apart and would see each other almost every day.

Harley was a very accomplished trainer. He had been doing this for almost 30 years and had sort of specialized in training racehorses. He was very good at what he did. One reason was because he was very thorough on every detail; very selective on any horse or endeavor he took on. Horse racing and horses were more important than anything else in his life. Harley was what everyone called a really nice guy.

John was also a pretty good guy by everybody's standards, but at the same time, he was called a horse trader. To most people who are familiar with the horse world, that kind of sends up a flag. But John was very good at horse-trading and had the ability to see potential and possibilities in horses that most people overlooked a lot of times. Harley had learned through their 20 years of knowing each other never to take John's ideas lightly. Many times John had come to him with some prospect, or some deal that Harley wasn't real keen on, and convinced Harley to get involved, and had been right every time. They both had a lot of respect for each other; John always came to Harley honestly and with the very best of intentions. Through the years, they had made a good team. John owned a small ranch and operated a little country store out in the middle of a big ranching community in New Mexico. He had been there a long time and was not a fly-by-night operator. Harley and John were close friends.

So this morning Harley is waiting on the end of his phone line for John to start a little sales pitch or tell him some big news item he has just heard about. The conversation kind of went nowhere for a minute or two, then Harley, trying to get it rolling, says, "I got a pretty big day today as I'm getting ready to leave for El Paso with two more colts for the track." He just thought he'd break John loose with the urgent reason he had called him at 5:00 a.m., but now he didn't seem to have that much to say. There was a little silence from John's end, and finally he asks in a soft voice, "What time you leavin?" It wasn't like John to beat around the bush. Usually he'd call and tell Harley what ever was on his mind right up front. But his calls were usually in the evening or around noon if he thought he could catch Harley in the house then. More often than not they had talked a lot of their deals over when they just happened to see each other on the street in town. There never had been this indication of urgency before. It's not that Harley wasn't interested in what his friend had on his mind, but he knew he must make John approach him as though any deal he had come up with; Harley wouldn't have the interest or the time. It just worked out better if he started it out on that kind of note. Finally, just to pin John down a little, Harley says, "I'm leaving around 9:00 o'clock." It was just like Harley had said he'd be leaving next week. John says, "Oh good. I got time to run over to your place. I'll see you in a few minutes," and he hung up the phone.

It was still very dark out and pretty chilly when to Harley's surprise, about 25 minutes after John had hung up the phone, he saw John's headlights rolling up the drive way and the lights behind him told Harley he was pulling his horse trailer.

John parked over in the area of one of the barns, made a fast trip to the front door, and let himself in without so much as a holler or a knock. He walked straight to the cupboard and got himself a cup and poured it full of coffee. Harley was reading the newspaper and still drinking his coffee. He just stared over the newspaper at John as if he was watching him pass by on a street corner down town. He had never seen John act like this before. Just to finally make some conversation, Harley said, "You know I'm glad you came over. I think you and me will dig some postholes today since we got this nice early start. I'll go to El Paso tomorrow." John, trying to keep from smiling, said, "I brought something over I want you to look at as soon as it gets daylight enough."

There was no more mention of his mission here as small talk went back and forth for a short time; daylight finally arrived. Just as mysteriously as John had been acting, Harley got up from his chair, rinsed out his coffee cup in the sink, put on his hat and coat, and started for the door. John gulped the last swallow from his cup, leaving it set there on the table, and was close behind Harley as they headed towards the pick-up and trailer.

John was almost trotting to keep up with Harley by the time they reached the trailer. He was hurrying to unlatch the end gate; Harley stood to the side so he could see what backed out of the trailer.

At last the news was out. A 3-year-old colt backed down off the trailer. John had him heavily blanketed so all you could see was the image of his two ears in the air and 2 big eyes blinking from behind a big fluffy hood. Jokingly, Harley said, "I'll take him. I need the blankets." John didn't smile at the intended joke as he led the horse up to the side of his pick-up and started unlatching the hood and blanket. Harley noticed a set of registration papers on the seat in John's pickup and reached in to get them. He said, "John! It says here these are Appaloosa papers." By this time, the blanket was pulled off and, sure enough, looking from side to side, stood a bewildered Appaloosa stallion. He was black and white, with very nice markings, including a real big pretty blanket with large spots all over his rear end; the dream of every Appaloosa breeder. But this colt looked starved, wormy, and his feet were badly neglected. One good thing in his favor was that he was gentle and had a pretty hide. Harley just stared at the horse, and John just stared at Harley. It seemed like an eternity of dead silence.

All of a sudden, John started his sales approach as if you had just walked in while he was in the middle of a long speech. He went on about how long he'd been trying to get this horse bought, and how much he'd seen happen to him.

The story was about an old man who had raised the colt and loved him, but had health problems. Because of his age, and his personal problems, he had neglected a number of his animals, including horses and dogs. Eventually, the old fellow passed away and there was no one at all to look after the animals; they really suffered from neglect. They had no feed or water and were left locked in filthy pens for days on end. Largely through John's efforts, all of the old man's animals had been confiscated, sold, or placed in good homes. John had bought this colt. He had always known that this horse was destined to end up with Harley. John recognized that the horse had great racing potential; it was perfect timing as a number of race tracks from Washington, to Nebraska, and across the Southwest were writing races for Appaloosas.

That was about as far as John got in his sales pitch, when Harley seized him by the shoulders and began his own speech. Harley was well known throughout the entire spectrum of his friends, business associates, veterinarians, and especially, John, that he did not have any use or time for Appaloosa horses. Several times he had bluntly said, "I don't believe they have any business being classified under the heading of horses." And had gone on to say, "I don't want them in any of my barns, or trailers, or taking up space on my ranch, or eating any of my feed."

He had not spoken those words loosely. Horses were his entire world, but he did not have any interest in the spotted horses. He considered them all losers. He said they waste your effort, time and money, and let you down every time you count on them. He always concluded, saying, "that's only my personal opinion, but there are more quarter horses and thoroughbreds than I will ever have a chance to train. I just don't have any reason to have any of them around me."

Harley now realized why John had been so secretive, and strange in his approach on this day. He was a little irritated about it all, and just wanted him to load his Appaloosa stallion back into the trailer and haul him off. But John stood like a rock and wasn't giving in. There was a whole bunch of talking, negotiating, debating, and even some pretty heated arguing, before a deal was finally reached.

Harley would go to work on the horse, train him, and run him at John's expense; John would pay all of the bills, and split any winnings 50-50 with Harley. Harley knew he had a huge rehabilitating job to do before anything happened; he was willing to bet that John would soon realize he was spending far more money than he had and would soon tire of the deal and sell the stallion to some pleasure rider. Not meaning any disrespect to anyone, but Harley could see a light at the end of the tunnel for himself, and a way out of this wreck that he was confident couldn't last more than a few months at the most.

He took the horse directly to one of his barns, where he would be placed in quarantine and isolation for a few weeks. John left Harley's yard in a cloud of dust, very happy with the way things had gone, and whistling a little tune as he drove down the road back to his store..

Harley started his usual day's work not near so pleased, but a little amazed at his old buddy John's faith in this poor, hard-luck horse he had pulled out of the wood work. The main ingredient in the whole set up was that all parties concerned knew, without any doubts, that Harley would do everything he agreed to and would give the horse every possible break available. That was the way Harley was.

He started with worming, a very careful feed ration, regular baths, and a lot of grooming. Blankets, blood work, additives and supplements, footwork, and, eventually, as the horse got stronger, careful and highly maintained riding. In the course of taking care of the horse, plus all of Harley's other commitments, the months passed quickly.

The Appaloosa stallion prospered, and bloomed; his personality was one of his strongest attributes. He became slick, filled out, and exhibited really good conformation and attitude. Several of Harley's exercise riders began commenting on the horse's abilities. They bragged about his speed and his strength. No one would have ever recognized him as the same horse that John left at the ranch back in October.

Now it was summer. In view of the way everything was going, even Harley began to look for a race to enter him in; he began to see he had a pretty good prospect here regardless of the color of his hide or his breeding. John had regularly paid high maintenance bills and met every demand Harley had made. Once again, it looked like a good deal. The only problem was that they had to break his maiden before he turned five-years-old. All of the races they could enter him in weren't apt to make them that much money. Appaloosa races were a little scarce. Once he broke his maiden (won a race) then he could run as long as he wanted to, but if it didn't happen by January 1st of his

5th year he could no longer go to the track. He was now 4 and had this year to get it done.

They found a race for him in June in Western Nebraska. It was a long ways to haul him, but he would command quite a bit of respect if he made a good showing. Harley had him tattooed and started in the gates; it looked like the stage was set. Harley's schedule with the other horses he was running kept him very busy. He had gone to a lot of trouble to get the Appaloosa into this race, and to arrange his time so that he could be there. But he did, and the day of the race arrived. Harley felt awkward involving himself in Appaloosa racing. But on this occasion, his old friend John was standing right beside him. He, too, had arranged his schedule so that he could be here at the horse's first race. As was his casual attitude, John expected to see big things happen.

He was not disappointed. When their race came up, they had the Appaloosa saddled, and paraded on to the track. He looked more like an old champion than a brand new starter. The horse was very calm and all business. Their jockey had boasted over and over that he didn't think there was a horse there that could run with him. At last, all of the horses were in the starting gates. There was that long silence and the eternal wait until the bell rang, the gates flew open, and the announcers voice sang out, "And they're off!"

John and Harley and many bettors heard little of what the announcer said from there on, as their horse broke well in the lead, gaining distance every stride until he crossed the finish line more than 2 lengths ahead of them all. He had just become a winner, a horse to contend with and, in their eyes, a smashing number one success. He was definitely on his way. He won a little more than $1000 with a number of bettors cashing in on their wagers. To say the least, there was a bunch of happy people there that day, including John and Harley and their associates, and one very proud Appaloosa stallion.

As weeks and months flew by, it was a repeat performance. John and Harley's Appaloosa won again and again, usually by big distances. He seemed very dedicated to attending to business. He became known as Harley's Step Child and various other pet names. Harley used him for pleasure riding, feeling that long days on the trail in big open country did a lot for his mind and kept him exercised better than daily runs around a track He became a popular rope horse at brandings, as well as roping competitions at rodeos. It seemed there was nothing he couldn't do.

He became the target of many people from as far away as away as Mexico wanting to match him—often for large sums of money. He never failed; he excelled, he conquered, and he won. Harley even got to where he tried to disguise him as a pony horse, leading quarter horses and thoroughbreds to the track. Harley would say to people who owned first-rate good running horses, "why, hell, I can outrun your horses with this old pony horse, and then he would do it. Very soon Harley's Step Child was the best known and most recognized horse on earth. He was loved, respected, and ridden by everyone from little 4th grade neighbor kids to cowboys, old ladies, and top name jockeys. All who came to see him admired and loved him, but probably the one most dedicated person in the Appaloosa horse's life was Harley himself.

John eventually sold the horse to Harley. The two of them had many great experiences and good times, from the beginning as the rescued, neglected victim, until he became the horse everyone knew and loved. Harley was beginning to make plans to retire him from racing and breed him to selected good mares around the country. He started really making big plans to produce more Appaloosa horses like him or maybe better.

One evening just after dark while Harley was at a racetrack, an old Mexican man approached him. He was also a very successful trainer and had a number of very good horses. He was quite wealthy and was someone Harley highly respected. He offered Harley a lot of money for his Appaloosa stallion and said that he too would retire the horse from the track and wanted him for his own personal horse to ride. He told Harley what a good life he would have and that he would graze mountain pastures, work cattle and just live out his life as an all around family horse and probably sire a few good colts.

He said, "I will pay you in cash this night for him." Harley, being careful not to offend the old man, declined his generous offer and said, "I believe with the things me and that old horse has done, I owe it to him to look after him and be there for him to spend his last days. We have come a long ways and I plan to stand by him." He explained that he was entered in one last big race and with that he was going to haul him home to his ranch where he would live out the exact same life that the old fellow had just described being his intentions. Finally, they departed, still good friends, but the old Mexican made Harley promise he would give it a lot of thought as it would be a very good way for the great Appaloosa stallion to spend his last days.

Harley agreed he would, but secretly felt in his heart that for all he and the Appaloosa had been through, they owed it to each other to stick together. He had to see this great horse through and be always in charge of his best interests. He felt he would have him there on his ranch until he died. And he was content with that thought. After all, the Appaloosa was still a young horse, really right in his prime. But he owed Harley nothing, and after all of the dark and dreary thoughts and statements Harley had made in his life against Appaloosa horses, Harley made up his mind he needed to remain the owner of this one.

As the date approached for his projected last race, Harley had stayed extremely busy and watched as it was getting harder and harder to find people who would run against his horse. He realized it was time to retire him and he kind of wished he hadn't entered him. What if something happened and he got out run or it crippled him. It would ruin his perfect career. He would look at this perfect specimen of a horse, his sure-of-himself attitude, and his incredible winning record; he felt he owed him the pleasure of one last big win.

The day of the race it was raining. The track was muddy. But the race would go on. Not much had ever slowed this horse down any. Betting was high, the purse was good, and Harley had hauled him a long ways to get here. He reminded himself of that day in Nebraska, when, together, they ran their first race, and what a rush all of that had been. This was like a repeat and Harley consoled himself with the fact that this would be the best way for his horse to go out, winning his last big race. Harley was up in the stands waiting and watching, the adrenaline flowing, the bell was ready to ring, and the announcer held his breath ready to start the fast and exciting second by second description of the race. And they were off! He ran down the track, mud exploding and flying on all the horses except the Appaloosa. He was in the lead by three lengths and gaining. The finish line was getting closer fast and the crowd was on their feet and yelling. It was deafening.

All at once there was an alarming snapping sound. It was heard above all of the other noise and immediately the crowd went quiet. The Appaloosa horse faltered and slowed to a stop in a few awkward and painful steps as the field of horses ran up on him, passed him on all sides like a huge herd of stampeding cattle, and went on to the finish line. The jockey bailed off at once, faltering and running hard himself, he and his horse finally stopped. The Appaloosa had snapped his front leg off completely right in the middle of the cannon bone—it was badly broken. He was in shock, staggered, and tried to turn and run. He was badly hurt and confused; finally, he stopped and held the leg off the ground, unable to move, as it dangled and swung in the air. He was breathing hard and sweating in the falling rainstorm—Harley had run to support and stand beside his horse. Tears were running down his face and he held the jockey in his arms. They both hugged and held the horse wherever they could get gathered around him; they both knew his racing career and probably his life was near the end. A compound fracture is not a pretty sight; the ambulance trailer was bearing down upon them. Many people in the crowd held their hands over their mouths and eyes in disbelief, not wanting to look. Many also wept. The winner of the race almost went unnoticed and the Appaloosa horse was loaded into the ambulance and hauled to his barn. It ended up being the saddest day many could imagine.

A sympathetic old veterinarian examined the broken leg over and over and finally determined there was no use, nothing could be done, and his advice was euthanasia. The race officials, usually pretty calloused to this type of thing, along with Harley, the jockey, and many of the spectators all watched in horror. Some people actually sobbed, as one by one they all realized the Appaloosa had run his last race and would be better off just to be put to sleep.

In a few minutes, it was done. The colt heaved one last big sigh and lay very still; the only sound was the rain on the roof. It was the end of a very great life, which happened to be the life a very special horse.

As Harley regrouped himself, he loaded his horse into his trailer with a lot of help from well-wishers and fans, and hauled him back to his ranch where he buried him beneath a nice stone. It was a tall grey grave marker. Oftentimes people from all over passed through and visited the horse's gravesite. In rainy weather, on cold winter days, or beautiful sunny summer days, they removed their hats and could hear the gates open, the roaring of the crowds, and see again a happier day, as a picture perfect black and white Appaloosa horse joins a field of very capable horses, and easily races across what would seem like the finish line into the beyond.

Visitors paid their respects to the horse that lies buried there and read the inscription on the grave marker placed there by the man they knew as Harley. He had coached and guided this horse to all of his wins and glories, and now is no longer there.

With lumps in their throats and misty eyes, they place their hats back on their heads, and walk away. "He was a good Appaloosa, who never let anyone down and, in fact, gave his last full measure to the very end."

HENRY
OLD COYOTE

bout 20 years ago I worked with a movie crew out of Billings, Montana. Among the approximately 200 white people and 400 Indians in the crew, there was none that left a bigger impression on me than one Henry Old Coyote.

Henry, at the time, was the Crow tribal historian. He was a very proud Crow and often told us very interesting stories of past and present day people of his Nation and the deeds they had each been known for.

One evening he was explaining to some of us about how much it meant to him being a Crow Indian, and how his being Crow was actually a religion with him and his people. To illustrate what he was telling us, he told the following story.

During World War Two, Henry was a crewmember on a bomber squadron, fighting the Japanese in the South Pacific. He said they had got hit and were shot down over heavily held Japanese territory. In a few days he and most of his crewmembers were captured and held prisoners by the Japanese.

They were taken to a compound where there were many Americans being held. He said they were all questioned each day, were given hardly any food, and beaten severely. Many of these captives were dying each day from torture, starvation, beatings, dysentery, or getting shot whenever they would be caught trying to escape. It began to look like the only way out for any of them was death.

After about 19 days of being moved from compound to compound and the extremely severe conditions he personally had undergone, Henry thought of his past life as he laid in a corner of the thatched hut that served as his cell, which he shared with quite a number of fellow captives. He had lost about 50 pounds from his normal weight of 160 pounds. He was badly bruised and cut from the beatings he had received. He felt lousy, had dysentery, and had eaten very little or nothing in many days. His spirit was totally drained, he could barely see at all due not only from the beatings, but also from the lack of food, water, and daylight, as they were made to stay inside most of the time. He prayed in the Crow way for Death to take him that very night. He was not only very certain that this was going to be the end result, but he actually felt he could never be the same again in any way. All that could be heard was the moaning of the dying. Some men who had totally given up or had lost their minds were sobbing, a few were praying. Some were still fighting with the last reserves they could muster up before they drifted off into a deep coma-like condition, which lasted a few hours before they finally passed away. The dead were buried in a fast and shallow dug mass grave right outside the compound. A grave with no markers, and in no particular place, and, which more than likely, would never be seen in that jungle by anyone again.

Mosquitoes swarmed over Henry and drained much

needed blood from his body. He had not the strength for several days to even feel them. He was hallucinating some, about the things he longed for at home. At times he saw himself as a little boy back in his beloved Pryor Mountain country with its large, high hills, good grass, sparkling streams, where he and his many friends rode their horses from one's home to another's in among the cottonwood trees to play games, fish, or swim. He saw again the cattle, horses, and wild life, which was such an important part of his memories of home.

There were also the old folks he saw in his mind that he missed, his neighbors, aunts, uncles, and most especially his grandfather and grandmother who were still living on their own ranch when he had gone away to fight for his country. But most of all, he missed his mother and father and brother. Once again a lot of those old experiences and pleasant memories passed through his terribly pained and troubled mind. On that sultry night, Henry felt that his God was very near and prayed for death to come that night and take him away from his extreme misery.

But suddenly, through the clouded and mixed up passing of his dreaming and hallucinating, he began to drift over into a vision. He saw himself as a much older man, maybe 10 or 15 years older than his actual age, and sometimes much older than that. He was healthy and had his normal weight back. He was some place he did not recognize, but he was sure it was somewhere in the Pryor Mountains. Then pretty soon a very clear dream or vision of a white house came into sight. There were many very vivid details such as a road passing between the house and a long shed. He saw large, tall cottonwood trees fully leafed out. Henry saw himself sitting on a type of hammock or swing, which was on a long porch that ran all along the front of that very pleasant white ranch-type house. He noticed that he appeared to be very well and very much at peace with himself in his vision.

In a little while the vision began to fade from his mind as he awoke from the deep sleep that he was deliberately trying to drive himself into. He began to realize once more all of the pain and misery he was living in, and as he tried to analyze what had just happened to him, he realized that he had received a very clear and definite message from his God. He was not going to die there in that terrible situation that he was now experiencing, and instead he would live through it and return to his loved ones, and his home land to live out his life.

The night passed as did several more, and Henry's vision remained strong in his mind. He actually began to realize a little more strength, and a very strong desire to remain alive grew. He began to work at conserving his strength and making what little food he got last. He did various exercises to maintain his strength, both physically and mentally. As days led into weeks and more of his comrades died, a few new prisoners arrived and there was talk from them that the war was coming to an end. The Japanese soldiers in charge of the prisoners seemed to be slackening up a little and at times seemed confused and almost too busy to keep up the rigid vigil they had maintained for so long. It began to look like escape was a possibility. If only he could find the strength when his chance came.

Well, eventually, Henry did escape along with some other soldiers, and they were soon reunited with American troops, as the war was coming to an end, and the ordeal was about over. He did make a full comeback and recovered from the whole encounter.

It had been more than 25 years since his release from the armed forces and his return to his homeland that Henry was telling us his story that warm summer evening. He didn't go into a lot of details about how he escaped, although I know that would be another interesting story in itself. But he did tell us that the very house he lives in today out there on Pryor Creek, in the Pryor mountains, where his horses graze right up to the door, and where his wife and children call home, along with their father, and where, on almost any Sunday afternoon, you can find Henry swinging on his porch swing and feeling very much at peace with himself, is that very same house that came to him in his vision that night so long ago in a far off land during the war.

INDIAN LOGIC

good many years ago, not long before the white man got involved with changing the American Indians' way of life, moving them to the reservations, and all of that part of history, there lived an old Indian in the western end of the United States. State lines, settlers, and boundaries didn't mean a whole lot to these people at that time. They took in the entire country, lived off the buffalo, the resources of the land, and did so very happily and successfully.

This man had been very successful in handling his own affairs and had become looked upon as chief, or at least head councilman, within his own tribe and society. All of his people knew and respected his judgment and often sought him out to help them with their problems and affairs.

He had raised three sons, also well respected, who valued their father's judgment as much as all the other people in their tribe.

One evening in late summer, the old Indian gathered his three sons and took them on a short ride into the hills. The summer had been a good one; the hills were very pleasant with a good grass crop, and many animals were all around them in plain sight lending a very secure and strong atmosphere that all four of the men could relate to and appreciate.

They rode out onto an outcropping of big flat rocks high above a grassy little valley surrounded by big cottonwood trees. They dismounted their horses as the sun was just starting to set in the west. The shadows were long with a lot of red and purple light reflecting onto the far away cliffs and mountains. The old man and his sons looked across the big expanse of country, enjoying their moment for a few minutes, then the old man began to speak.

He spoke in his native tongue, with the usual amount of sign language, and he said, "I have been very blessed throughout my life, and I now know my time is short for the Great Spirit came to me in a dream. I have seen old times and old friends who have gone to the spirit world and soon I will join them again. I have not much to give you my sons, other than my herd of horses which I have spent my life breeding and building. They are very special to me and I am looking forward to leaving them to you. It is my desire that you three will split the herd evenly among you, and I want you to do it this way." He faced his oldest son squarely and said, "I would like you to gather my herd when I have passed over the divide. Pick your equal share first, taking all of the ones you choose, until you have counted your total number. You are my oldest son, and you and I have spent many times at war, hunting, and traveling."

Then to the other two sons he said, "After your brother has picked his total herd count, you being the next oldest will pick yours first, and then the youngest will pick until you have each totaled the same number of horses. It is very important," he explained, "that all three of you remain loyal to one another and treat each other right. There are to be no hard feelings; only a grateful happiness when you have divided them evenly."

When the old man had finished his talk there was a great silence as darkness was coming down upon them. They were all in agreement and were very happy, yet saddened by his message as they rode back home.

Sure enough, in about 10 days, the old man rode out to one of his favorite places and passed away just as he had predicted. For a few days there was mourning and a show of much respect for the loss of a beloved man who had served his family and his people very well.

On the given day, just as the sons had been instructed, they each picked a couple of their best friends and rode out into the far away hills to gather their father's horses. They were close and very friendly as they brought the herd in to the same little valley to hold them while the three brothers divided the horses exactly as their father had directed.

The first thing they noticed was that there was a total of twenty head and they knew that twenty could not be equally divided by three. One brother would be short and would only get six horses. After a short discussion, the youngest brother began to get a little irritated and hostile. He felt that the oldest brother getting first pick, should be satisfied with six and that would leave seven apiece left over for the two younger brothers. They started arguing and getting mad at each other even though they had been warned by their father not to let this happen.

Finally, the oldest son said, "Let us have our old friend the medicine man come here. He will know how to handle this." They all agreed with him.

The old medicine man had been a close friend of theirs and of their father's; he had seen many winters. He was quite stern and indisputably wise. As he rode up, he could immediately see the problem and became concerned. He said, "I am as old as your father, and I, too, am not long for this world. I am going to turn my own horse in with those of yours and that will give you twenty-one head to pick from." It was obvious to all that he was very old and stiff and his old horse was quite the same. But he very willingly unsaddled him, dropped his saddle there among the tall grass, pulled the bridle off of his old horse, and stood back as he watched him trot out to join the bunch of very fine horses the boys were now going to split.

Then he said, "I will need one horse for my medicine." All three boys readily agreed. The old man went on, "You boys make your choices, and I'll take the last horse left standing for my fee."

Immediately they divided their horses as planned and all three boys were happy again. As the youngest son went to pick his last horse, he noticed that one was a very fine bay colt his father had been very proud of, and the one who stood beside him was the medicine man's tired old worn-out horse. The son looked troubled and said, "It is my choice, and I want to take the bay, but that leaves you only your horse that you donated to us. I really don't want him." The medicine man said, "Take the one you want, my only request was that I take one horse. I said the last one standing. If he is the one, then I will take him." So the boy took the nice bay colt, and all were satisfied with their selections.

Each of the three sons got their friends to help them drive their herds off towards their respective homes. As they were doing this, the old medicine man caught up his own horse and saddled him up. He climbed on him and rode off towards his home. As he rimmed out up in the rocks climbing out of the little valley, he stopped on a ridge and noticed the sun was getting down in the far away western sky. Looking out across the magnificent hills, he could see each son and their friends trailing their newly acquired herd of horses up a little draw heading home; each feeling good and happy that all had gone well.

The old medicine man searched the sky and knew he could feel the presence of his old friend, and hoped, that from some far away vantage point, he had seen what had been done and was pleased. The old man thought to himself how important it is that we don't get so greedy, we make ourselves look foolish. He petted the neck of the old horse he had ridden so many times and for so many miles. Admiring his long neck and his old familiar ears, and he felt very proud to have this one.

KELLY'S DAD BUYS A NEW SADDLE

boy and his dad go through a lot of different trials, realizing breeches of different emotions and occasionally add an unpleasant memory, but most of the stories about the trials are unforgettable, just proud, happy, moments forever remembered as times of dedication, loyalty and much love. Most of these stories are very personal, although often expressed as pleasant and affectionately told stories by one or the other whenever either of them may away or is no longer around.

Once in a while a boy and his father become very close and spend quite a nice portion of their lives together; the father living out of his life as the older man, and the son realizing every day how proud he is of his father's wisdom, experiences, and judgment for all he has been through. The son becomes involved in the family business and the father gets to enjoy the son that he raised to manhood. In his own heart, he can enjoy each day the proud, happy feelings he'd always hoped for as he watched his son become a very good man. Each thank the other very often though not always verbalized.

Kelly was the son in this case, and he had turned out pretty well. He was a good cowboy, rancher and general businessman. Cattle and ranching had been his life, and he had owned and leased a pretty good scope of ranches, some of which he would always keep and manage to insure a steady income. This allowed him to branch out on a few side ventures, such as managing other people's places, or buying and selling a little real estate. Now and then he'd buy and sell herds of cattle and horses, which kept him extremely busy, and was often quite lucrative.

As Kelly wore on into his middle-age years, he had been pretty successful, all the while thanking his father for his good advice, teachings, and the discipline he'd taught him. His father, now older and semi-retired, had proudly watched his son's progress and was grateful for his successes and often thought how proud he was of his son.

One day, in his travels, Kelly met and befriended

a famous saddle maker whom he had known of for a long time. The saddle maker had taken a job with a big company and worked for them a number of years, gaining a lot of recognition for his name, but not reaping much of the financial benefits for himself. At the time Kelly met him, he had just gone on his own and was opening his first shop and needed some orders. He told Kelly he had designed a saddle built especially for either cutters or maybe reiners with just enough changes to work very well for real cowboys to ranch in, cattle in, or gather wild horses. He felt he had a rare product that would really sell if he could get a few out to the mainstream of horse breakers and cowboys.

He told Kelly, "If you would order one of these from me, I'll build it for you for $1700. I really need $2200, but to get started, I'll build you this one for $1700." Kelly, feeling confident, and a little bit flush at that moment, ordered the saddle, offered his preferences, and promised to be back in about six weeks to get his new saddle.

For a busy man, time goes fast, and before Kelly could believe his eyes, he was again walking through the front door of his friend's new shop to pick up his new saddle. When he first saw it, he was so delighted, as was the saddle maker who built it. After writing him a check, he finally got it loaded up and was ready to leave the shop. He promised to try to sell more just like it as he went out and about the country side. He drove away and could hardly wait to get to his ranch to try it out.

A new saddle isn't fun or easy to break in, but Kelly rode this hard from the first day he got home with it. The more he rode it, the better he liked it, and, in a few weeks, he realized it truly was special; he really liked it. He had ridden a couple of bucking horses in it and had also roped a few big cows out of it. He decided it was surely built to last and was long on comfort and service.

He was traveling to one of his other ranches when had to pass by his father's house. He decided to stop and show his new saddle to his dad, because he knew he would really appreciate it and would also be pleased to see who had made it. He had known this saddle maker for a good many years and would be happy to see he had gone out on his own. Kelly's dad had given him his first saddle many years ago, which he still owned, but now he kind of side-lined it in lieu of riding this nice new one.

Kelly's dad, after greeting his son, and a little fast and usual visiting, finally got out to the truck and saw the saddle. He was highly impressed with it, and after noticing Kelly's enthusiasm, really like it. So much so, that he finally said, "Kelly, will you go order me up one of these?" This really made Kelly feel good about it, though he kind of felt to himself that his dad really didn't need such an expensive new saddle at his age. Although he did still ride and, in fact, quite often helped Kelly with much of his work. Kelly promised to stop right away and order the new saddle, and when he tried to get his dad's prefer-ences, he was told, "Just have it made identical to this one. This one is just great."

So within days, it was done. The saddle was ordered exactly like the first one, but Kelly had said maybe you better put a 16" tree in this one as dad is a much larger man than me. That was to be the only change. All except for one the saddle maker had come up with. He said,

"Kelly, I made your first one for $1700-that was my deal. This one, and all other orders, I must get my full $2200." Kelly struggled with this news and wondered if he should call his dad and ask him if this raise in price would change his mind. He finally just decided to go ahead and have him make the saddle. The saddle maker told him he'd have to put down a deposit which Kelly agreeably did-$750-the balance to be paid on the day he picked it up.

Once again, he left the shop very happy and excited and so was his friend, the saddle maker. But as Kelly drove away, he arrived at a thought that he really felt good about. He decided to give his dad the saddle in appreciation for the things he had done for him throughout their lifetime. Although it occurred to him his dad, being as proud as he is, probably wouldn't accept it as a gift. But for the next few days, Kelly entertained the idea and then would catch himself thinking, he really didn't have the money to do it right now. He felt he needed to buy some other things right now as expenses were so high, but it was just one excuse after another. He batted the idea back and forth, on the one hand, feeling really good about doing it, but, then, on the other hand, realizing he couldn't afford it.

This went on until the day rolled around to pick up the second new saddle. As Kelly walked into the shop that morning, he fully realized things were quite different than a few weeks before. He was pretty broke. He had had a lot of expenses, some set backs, and the idea of him just blowing off $2200 because he wanted to give his dad the saddle was out of the question. He finally agreed with himself, that that just wasn't going to happen today. But he did go ahead and wrote out the check to cover the balance.

The saddle, which turned out to be an exact duplicate of the first one, was every bit as nice, if not nicer. The saddle maker, Kelly, and his dad were on a roll.

Kelly took his father's new saddle and headed for his dad's house with it. All of the way he cursed and worried that he ought to just give it to his dad when he got there, but this was $2200-he was going to just give away! He drove through the big gate and pulled up in front of his father's house. In all of their happiness and excitement, Kelly felt very awkward knowing he intended to ask his dad if he would reimburse him for the cost, he tried to ease the question to him, and started out by explaining to the older man how the saddle had now cost $2200. He just mentioned this, so when he finally had to ask for the check, his dad would know how large to make it. His words almost went unnoticed as his dad touched and admired the new saddle. Kelly tried to remember if it was the first new one his dad ever had. Finally, Kelly's dad said, "Come in to the house, son, it's cold out here." They filled two cups with coffee and Kelly's dad called out to his wife, who was every bit as excited about it all as her husband. "Momma, will you write Kelly a check here for $2200." She immediately sat down and happily wrote out the check. Kelly's stomach cramped—he wanted so badly to just give his dad the saddle. He took one long pull on his cup of coffee, and finally just made himself say, "No, mom, this saddle is for dad, and I don't want to be paid for it. I'm so happy he likes it—I want to give it to him. Do not pay me for it." All of a sudden he totally understood that the price of that saddle was a long, long way from any kind of pay back that he could give his father for their lifetime together, and for all he had done for him over the years. But neither of his parents said anything until she had handed her husband the check. Kelly's dad placed it his hand and said, "Son, you and I both know I don't need that new saddle. But mom and I noticed how much you liked the one that you have, and we both felt with all that you are doing, you could easily use another, and that is our gift to you. You must take back the cost of it and take the saddle with you. Both parents beamed proudly and their eyes showed that they had received more in return than the pitiful $2200 they had spent.

Several years later, Kelly stood in my yard showing me some horses he wanted to sell, and in his conversation had called my attention to the two identical saddles cinched up on those horses. He told me the story, and as he went to walk past the big paint horse wearing the saddle with the 16" tree, Kelly stopped, squared around, and admired the saddle. He seemed, for a moment, to be in a world of his own, then he reached out, pulled a couple of short jerks on the strings, looked over at me and patted the horse on the hip as he walked on by. He said over his shoulder, "It still embarrasses me every day to think how much I argued with myself about doing that for them and how willing and easily they did it for me. It taught me a lesson far more expensive than both of these saddles." And I know I knew what he meant.

RUBBY MEETS
BIG EDD

It used to be that all of the bigger ranches in the country needed extra hands during the busier seasons, like calving, irrigating or feeding, and again at shipping time. In each case, it would be seasonal and short-time employment, maybe lasting only a month or so. There seemed to always be a steady stream of cowboys coming by to take over these jobs. Many times transients from all over the country would appear to apply; like they knew the job would be coming up, and they wanted to get it. Having had no experience with animals or ranch life whatsoever, many knew nothing at all about the country or the type work they'd have to do.

Quite often a lot of them were merely broke, needed to find some way to acquire a few dollars to feed a bad alcohol habit, and only planned to accept the jobs long enough to obtain a bottle or two of wine and then they would be gone. They were of little help to anyone, including themselves. So, as a rule, many busy ranchers would prefer to try to hiring someone who came to them rather then going into town to look for help. More than likely the ones in town wouldn't turn out to be any better than the one standing at their door. But most of the time, there was a steady turn over due to lack of qualifications. Just when a rancher in need was convinced he would never hire another total stranger who came begging for work, one would show up who was excellent for the job; maybe a better description would be at least qualified and very adequate. Then he would open the door again for the next several lesser applicants; the rancher hoping one of them would turn out to be like that last guy.

Every rancher had his list of old standbys, usually neighbors, relatives of friends, or acquaintances who had some how got involved and had spent many years, or even most of their lives, working for the same ranch. They would often disagree over methods, ideas, or wages and, at times, cuss and condemn each other. But then turn around and stick up for one another in some crisis or neighborly dispute. Most of the time, in their own way, they were very sincere and loyal to each other.

Rubby came under this category. He was born and raised in a very small settlement known as Lenney's Mont. It was really just a little railroad town where section hands for the old Milwaukee Railroad were stationed. Thousands of sheep and cattle were shipped by train from their stockyards over a good many years. There were at least three to five families who lived there permanently in houses provided by the railroad and were employed by the Milwaukee to keep up the tracks, the fences, clear the snow out of the switches, and general maintenance. They had about 15 miles of track each way in and out of Lenney's to maintain, and also be on hand to feed, load, and care for all of the livestock being shipped in or out; as well as feed, all kinds of machinery, and supplies acquired by those ranches in that area.

Most of the families consisted of young boys who, as they began to grow up, went out and took jobs on those same ranches and were counted on as very reliable hands. Each rancher would train them as to how he wanted things done and those boys, being strong and eager to work, were the answer to the ranchers' needs.

Rubby's dad kept the railroad running, his mother kept a happy household, and raised all of his baby brothers and sisters to adults. Rubby became one of the mainstays on the vast Voldseth Ranch. Once in a while hiring out for a summer, or a few months to Cad Rosted, or another neighbor or two, but he always migrated back to Voldseth. By the time he was in his forties, he had put on quite a bit of weight and sometimes supporting a pretty healthy drinking habit. His main intent in life, and seemingly the biggest accomplishment of his 40 plus years, was to become accepted as one of their steady and permanent fixtures. Their ranch became his second home. He knew what they needed done and he did it pretty much in his own way and time. Nobody paid much attention to him; they just always knew Rubby would be there and the ranch would be just fine.

The older Voldseth brothers, George and Norman, had run things on the ranch throughout their lifetime. Norman, who had no kids, just accepted it when George's family took over all the operations after George passed away. All through those years, Rubby had attended many Voldseth family gatherings, and had experienced all of their private glories, through both good and bad years, for more than two generations of ranching. He had shared many meals and lots of whiskey with them, but he always remained their steady ranch hand. When his own parents and other family members passed away, he became more attached to the Voldseth family.

Many other employees came and went. Some stayed a month or two or all summer, some a week or two, and once in a while, a few wouldn't last more than a day or so. But Rubby would just laugh; he knew what was expected of him. There wasn't much left in old Rubby's makeup to make him appear like any kind of a problem or threat to any one. He seemed to do his job in an almost ineffective way. Once in a while he'd complain, or seem a little disgruntled over things, but mostly he just did what he could and not much more.

Then one day someone hauled in one of those new job seekers who would show up every so often. His name was Edd and he'd spent most of his life in and around Dillon, Montana. He claimed he had ranched there all of his life. That was his first boast. His second boast was that he had once been a pretty progressive prizefighter. He sometimes mentioned having sparred with Floyd Patterson. But among all of his often- heard boasts, he never once said how he had arrived clear down here in our country looking for this ranch job. The other thing that kind of helped to back up the stories of his past was his looks. He was a giant of a man, and age was a definite factor in his looks. He moved rather slowly and was kind of stiff in his gait. His shoulders were not broad, but very drooped; he moved and looked like he weighed 400 pounds! Other noticeable traits were a few missing teeth, a scarred and badly bent nose, and a hairline that went clear down, if not right over the top of his two bushy eyebrows. Very little of his forehead showed at all, just enough to let you see it was very sloped.

He was constantly talking about fights he had been in, and people he had been forced to beat up. Every job he set out to do was set aside while he explained, to anyone who would listen, all about his past fights, being hauled off to jail for some brawl, and about how he beat up the cops/highway patrolmen in the Sheriff's office. He seemed to be trying to impress upon everyone that you'd better treat him pretty careful or you could be his next casualty.

Big Edd, as everybody started calling him, ended up having to work a lot with Rubby. Rubby started explaining to everyone that he found himself doing most of the work while he listened to Big Edd tell over and over about all of his past deeds and conquests. Rubby went on each day for about two weeks doing both his and Big Edd's work and not paying much attention at all to Big Edd. Rubby would laugh easy and often; that was his main reaction to about everything that happened to him.

Saturday night finally rolled around and everybody on the Voldseth Ranch ended up in town at the Mint Bar. This, like a lot of the other things that kept those old ranches going, had been happening for many years. For lack of anything better going on, everyone from all of the ranches around would gather at the bar. Often there would be a little old country band providing good listening and dance music. There was always an endless supply of beer and whiskey to break up the boring daily routine and help create a very enjoyable time until the next morning.

Some of the people had formed into little private groups, while others organized two or three tables into a circle, and began telling stories of the past weeks or tales from over the years, really enjoying the moment.

Rubby was sitting among seven or eight of his closest friends, and Big Edd was standing behind Rubby's chair just outside the circle. He didn't know anyone, and no one was interested in hearing about his past exploits. There was a lot of talking and much laughter. Finally, Rubby excused himself for a minute and went to the restroom. When he returned, he walked up to his group and found Big Edd sitting in the chair he had just vacated.

Rubby, being somewhat polite, stood for a second so as not to interrupt someone telling a story. Edd just stared straight across the room like he hadn't noticed Rubby's return at all. Directly, Rubby says, "Excuse me, Edd, but you are in my chair." Edd just politely answered, "I'm sorry, Rubby, but I believe I saw you get up and leave, and as there was no one sitting here, I sat down."

The smile disappeared from Rubby's face at once, and his face turned very red. A terrible look of rage just consumed him; his eyes turned rock hard all at once. Rubby said, "You may be the toughest guy in here, but this is B.S.!" Without another word, he reared back and swung with a wide right that caught Big Edd along side of his face. Edd flew out of the chair, tipping it over, and landed on his side. His face burned into the hardwood floor, one side bleeding from where Rubby's roundhouse swing had landed, and the other side burnt and peeled from smacking the floor. Rubby had no idea what to expect when Edd picked himself up among a lot of spilled

155

beer, but he probably expected to be in the fight of his life. Most of the laughter and talk stopped instantly, and the bartender prepared to take steps to stop the fight and protect his bar. The band just kept right on playing. But Edd got up awkwardly and, acting kind of dazed, just sort of eased his way out of the bar. Talk started up again and Rubby remounted his chair that he had set back in place again. No one noticed when Edd left the bar, or the town, but it was pretty noticeable when he didn't show up for work either Sunday or Monday morning. He supposedly returned to one of his old jobs back in Dillon more than 200 miles away.

A few people tried to bring the story up to Rubby the next day, but unlike Big Edd, Rubby didn't see anything in it to brag about; electing instead to repeat an old story that had been told many times before. It was about the big snowstorm of 1948, thirty- years earlier, and how tough that winter was. Besides, he had to go attend to his job.

"ONE GUY'S OBSERVATION"

Bill moved to Arizona in the early '50s. He wasn't much more than twenty-years-old and had beside him his brand new wife, who wasn't even quite that old. He started out on the old Diamond A Ranch, in particular, a ranch just north and east of Benson. It was a new ranch to the old conglomerate, and they were right then in the process of gathering several hundred head of cattle that had really gone wild and were considered ungatherable. They were just thrown in on the deal and came along with the ranch. The sellers thought there were only between fifteen to twenty-five head out there in those hills that ran along the San Pedro River with her solid clumps of mesquite trees. The new owners finally realized they had inherited several hundred cattle as a bonus in the purchase price.

It fell to Bill to spend his time trying to capture as many cattle as he could. After a few weeks on the job, he began to understand that every time he topped a hill while on horseback, the cattle spotted him, noticed his dust, and realized they were being invaded. They fled exactly like the Apaches had done when they were being rounded up from this same range less than one hundred years before. Bill told me several times how he laid out and stalked these cattle on foot, following them into water traps and blinds he had built, until he had captured over two hundred head. Eventually, they got them all and shipped them back to restock the ranch along with the more modern cattle of the day.

He had grown up in Texas, and starting out young, worked on a few ranches and proved himself to be highly responsible. It was always in the back of his mind that one day he would work for himself—he was sure that it would be ranching. He rode broncs and broke horses. He became an avid horseman, learned the entire cow business, built his scruples, and learned that the only rewards in life are derived from very hard work and lots of long hours.

In the course of his pursuit of success, Bill ran across

an extra nice piece of land just to the west of Benson. It was pretty good-sized and part of a ranch known as Mescal, which was just starting to be subdivided. Only a few houses and small ranchettes were being built close to the highway, but they were enough to stop the ranch's regular operation. Bill managed to lease all the land that wasn't settled and started his own operation from this fabulous piece of native pasture. This lease that he negotiated with a fair number of relatives of the original owners, lasted for more than thirty-five years. Bill leased more land all over Arizona, parts of Texas and New Mexico, and also sold many cattle. He ran a successful operation that produced a variety of herds from his own cattle. He became very well known throughout the country to both old and new operators and in many circles of cow ranchers.

I came here to Arizona in the early 1980s and became an acquaintance of Bill's. The man I met, and grew to know, was a fellow strictly self-contained, self-supporting, and never at an end for new ideas or efforts. He would appear at the coffee shop by 4 AM, or earlier, with a horse already saddled and loaded, ready to head for one of his pastures. Sometimes he had a hand that would try to help and keep up with him. If you ever went to work for Bill, the one thing you wouldn't need would be your bed! Every day ran on over into tomorrow and was still going on yesterday. But when the job ended, he would pay you very well. If you were reasonably good help and willing to work, Bill would use you often. If you were no help, or didn't want to work, he had absolutely no respect for you at all. Most all of his words and actions reminded you of old timers from the past now gone.

In no way are we trying to account for Bill's successes, failures, personal accomplishments, or of his efforts in this sketchy report of Bill's life story. But we are often reminded of the day when he, on his own, came and asked us if we would like to lease his Mescal pasture to run our brood mares on. He felt that he was going to quit using it, as there were too many nesters on the property making it too small for him to use. While he didn't mention it, he knew he was experiencing health problems. We had long considered Bill a very good friend, but will always be most grateful for his thoughtfulness and efforts in helping us to acquire the pasture; once it was done, he went home and began to doctor his failing health. He fought his disease the very same way he fought for life, and for his success over the past years in the cow business. We started using and enjoying the pasture right away. For eight years we harvested our colt crops and seen them born and raised to end up all over the country as ranch horses, pleasure horses, and, occasionally, a few as show horses.

During the time we were worrying and caring about how Bill and his family were handling the medical process of helping him to survive and, in fact, live; we were also worrying if it was going to rain or not, would the grass carry our mares or burn off, did we have enough water, were we over grazing, were the mares in foal, were we saving their babies, and lots of other important questions.

I pulled into the pasture one morning to check and feed the mares, as feed had been getting short. It was a one of those bright and warm sunny mornings. We'd had enough rain lately that the hills were showing a rich growth of new green, some good grasses, some weeds, but feed. Off to my left, and out there in front of me in the pleasant sunshine, I could count at least a half-a-dozen new little foals, anywhere from two-days to two-months-old, running and playing and nursing. They were growing into healthy and very fine prospects for some optimistic horse buyer. It was an easy morning to be there, and no matter what pressures and problems one might have, you couldn't help feeling optimistic. In the morning sunshine, it was very pleasant to see thirty-head of brood mares all sunning themselves, nosing through the fresh new growth of green grass and partly blooming fillarees; their babies playing at their sides and promises of more new babies to come. Also on that morning, I had received word that Bill had been moved to the hospital because he had become that sick. His serious battle with cancer was definitely worsening.

As I stopped to think and reason out all of the thoughts going through my mind, it occurred to me that everything in this world is relevant.

I thought of the man who, for more than thirty-five years, had made a very successful business here with his cattle. I'm positive he may have spent some days standing exactly where I was, feeling exactly the same thoughts as me, as he watched little Brahma calves bunt and nurse at their mama's side, seen them grow big, as he pondered his future and well-being. On any given day during that thirty-five-year span, different people may have considered Bill a crook or a good friend, a villain or a hero; much like a strong wind coming across those hills in that pasture may be praised by some for running the windmill or blowing in a rain storm, while being condemned by others for breaking the mesquite beans off the new growth on the trees or bringing cold weather to the newborn babies or drying out the moisture.

The man was making a living by furnishing cattle for truckers to haul, giving hay growers a feed market feedlots, cattle to feed, and giving families the greatest food there has ever been. At the same time, his cattle were eating the gardens and flowers of the new residents, or were being hit on the streets and highways by cars or trucks, and sometimes Bill had to order the neighbors to stay off his property, at times causing some ill feelings.

Meanwhile this beautiful pasture which furnishes feed, shelter, and a perfect place for these animals to call home and enjoy the freedom of space, also produces cactus which can and does cripple them, poisonous plants which can cause bloat or death, and burrs that tangle in their hair, stick in their hides, and irritate their eyes.

One day, not so long ago, I myself might have looked forward to having a job with Bill, because he would pay me well, and I could ride and train a colt that I could then sell for an income. He often had work when no one else did. Now I consider myself very busy and even in need of someone to work for me. Bill has done his thing and is trying to realize a few more days of quality life. In every direction we see the remains of last year's grass that has gone dry and withered up; old mesquite beans lie scattered around while the new green ones are much in demand by the animals.

When any of us go looking for helpers, there are some who could carpenter, some who could build fence, and some who could ride a bronc. But then there are also those who have never learned to operate a shovel or hammer and sometimes they might be too hung over or not even interested enough to leave their house.

Out in the pasture rabbits add entertainment and amusement to the landscape, vultures that thrive only on animals that may have become down or are dead, coyotes eating newborn babies, and one might even be the horse you ride to gather on or get your work done.

No matter what species of life we are, we have our days when we are productive and days when we wear away and become pretty much a has-been or a hazard.

If we are of the land, there is a time when we are the difference in feed or perhaps a fire hazard or, in the case of the tumbleweed, just a plain nuisance, having been good feed in its youth.

We must never forget to appreciate the good times of the past. For one day we may become unknown or of little value, be us flesh and blood, stem and leaf, a hay meadow or even a parking lot. We may be a refreshing well one day and the next day a dry hole in the ground. Nothing and no one is for very long; we will each have our good and bad days.

In the next few days, Bill went on to his last reward. A few other old friends have also gone on and we have met some new ones, with still others yet to meet.

The pasture is going on just as life goes on. There is another exciting group of foals just growing up and getting ready to leave their mothers to become what they are going to be.

We wait and pray for rain and a few more days of quality life—everything is relevant.

SMOKEY AND JOE

lmost any direction North, South, East, or West of the area surrounding the site of the town known as Twodot, Montana, is considered excellent ranch country. The grasses that grow in this part of Montana are as good as anywhere on earth. Shelter from the severe winters is provided by rough breaks, lots of patches of cottonwood trees, and willows all backed up by plenty of line running water and hay-bearing meadows of both native grass hay and alfalfa. Settlers from more than 200-years ago recognized the land's potential and made good use of this part of the country and the natural resources for their herds of sheep, cattle, and horses.

Directly south of Twodot are large grassy flats that rise on up from the Mussellshed River Valley to gradually rougher and steeper hills for a few miles. Then all at once, you see before you a big country with high, far reaching hills, not tall enough to qualify for mountains, but standing as sentinels surrounding the entire lower valley. This range of hills spans East to West about 30-miles before turning into the Crazy Mountains to the South, that extend as high as 11,000'. The tall hills are named; Twodot Butte, Black Butte, Coffin Butte, Rattlesnake Butte, and others.

Each peak has a name of its own due to its location, shape, or characteristics, respectively.

One of the oldest and best known ranches in the Twodot area was the Moore Livestock Co. which started out almost 200-years ago with the members of the early day Moore family putting together this fabulous ranch. Eventually, after having raised famous herds of sheep and cattle, they handed the ranch down to their sons, Perry and George Moore, who, like their parents, built and raised more famous herds of sheep and cattle while in the process of raising their own families who they hoped would follow in their footsteps.

During this period, while Perry and George were operating the ranch and making history in this wonderful area of Montana, a different group was making history of another kind all around a good portion of America with a famous horse known as Steel Dust. Ranchers, horsemen, and almost everyone who ever dreamed of owning a horse was breeding, buying or acquiring one of these Steel Dust sired horses. His descendents set records and had people standing in amazement at the speed and abilities they each possessed. These people were crossing them with whatever breed of horses they had around and, as a result, this new breed would one day become the biggest forerunner to the American Quarter Horse.

Like true stockmen, the Moores negotiated with the group and came up with a stallion, a true descendent of the Steel Dust line. They turned him out on their ranch, which included almost the entire Twodot Butte. They had a band of mares, which ranged from wild mustangs, thoroughbreds, Indian ponies, and probably some draft breeds out on the range with the stallion.

When their mares foaled in the spring and early summer on the thousands of acres of strong grass; coyotes, wolves, and mountain lions witnessed their births right along with birds, deer, gophers, rabbits, antelopes, and even rattlesnakes—all were to become their stable mates. The foals became familiar with lightening, thunder, mosquitoes, badger holes, and old barbed wire from the day they were born. The one thing they weren't familiar with in those days was man—until the day they were finally rounded up and brought into the big ranch corrals to be cut off from their mothers. They would get a little roughed up, experience an acquaintance routine through branding, and go through a couple of days of fast handling until they were fully weaned. They were then turned back out to the open range to mature into two-or three-year-olds. They'd be gathered again, start their breaking years, and begin their careers as cow horses. For a good many years, regular hands at the Moore Ranch rode the sons and daughters of these horses; many became household words in the community as they discussed and talked about their cow-cutting skills, or their ability to buck, or whatever became their best field. None of it made much difference in those days no matter how they went about it, those boys rode them and got their work done.

The Moores and their horses endured WWI, the Depression, and the dry years of the late 1920s and '30s. One day, towards the end of the 1930s, a man named Buster was helping to work some sheep at the Moore

Ranch and noticed a pair of colts, one a black two-year-old, the other a little brown yearling. He talked to the Moores about the possibility of buying these two wild little horses, descendents of Steel Dust on the top side and a couple of little Indian mares being each of their dams. They were half-brothers on their Sire's side. Eventually, a deal was made, and what seemed like a small price for a horse in those days, was quite a large sum for Buster to come up with at that time. Once he had bought them, he then had to figure out how he was going to get them gathered and brought home to his place in Twodot. While he was writing out the check for the colts, Buster had already decided to name them Smokey and Joe. As a baby, Smokey, now two-years-old, had been bitten by a stallion on his neck and it had left a big blemish. As he matured, it was hidden under his mane and never seemed to bother him any. Joe, the little brown yearling, was blemish free. He was a little smaller than the black, but he was very wise. Neither horse ever weighed more than 800 pounds.

Buster was a young family man trying to get established on his own ranch and had two young boys, about three- and five-years-old, at this time. He bought the two little horses with his boys in mind and, as it turned out, by the time the horses had lived out their lives, they had become every bit as much a part of the family as Buster, his wife, their two older boys and the two younger children, another boy and their only daughter that he and his wife raised. As the family grew, so did their love for Smokey and Joe.

As soon as they were each old enough, Buster found

a couple of young teen-age boys to start breaking them in and riding them. Smokey bucked each of the two boys off a few times, but then quit and went to work from his first day of training. Before long, Frank, who was five-year-old, claimed Smokey and started riding him everywhere. John, the three-year-old, laid full claim to Joe and, in a very short time, the four were inseparable.

At first there were the starting out years when the boys rode around the corrals and then in and outside of the fenced yard. The horses learned to be gentle and patient with the boys and they, in turn, learned how to ride horses with a lot of potential. As time went on, the boys got old enough to run errands on Smokey and Joe; they even developed chores to do on them, like checking on the sheep and bringing in the milk cows. The horses and the boys began to mature fast. It wasn't long until the whole community saw a lot of Smokey, Joe, Frank, and John. Every bit of riding, each errand, and every duty performed on horseback was monitored and highly disciplined by Buster and his wife, Rose. The boys were taught not to show off, not abuse the horses, and to respect all of the neighbors' properties. There were also a fair number of neighborhood kids who all had some kind of horses to ride. They were older ranch horses that included Arabians, Shetlands, thoroughbreds, mules and Indian ponies. Everyone respected each other and their horses.

While all of those kids in that neighborhood were learning to be horsemen, they were also learning responsibility, all kinds of things about nature, the sights and topography of the land, and above all to appreciate, respect, and love horses. As they got a little older, they all learned to feed, groom, and even shoe their own horse. At first Frank, being the oldest, did most of this for him and John, but by an early age they both had learned to do it all themselves.

There became a purpose and an attitude for both horses and boys. No doubt that there were mistakes made and plenty of mischief that happened between the four of them. Those two little horses had matured into fantastic role models and teachers to that pair of boys growing up on a small Montana ranch. As the years passed, the boys became teenagers and learned to break other horses, both their own and for the neighbors, and were soon employed by all of the neighboring ranches to help with all kinds of work. Quite often this included riding jobs, and while Smokey and Joe had each done plenty of that, too—the boys got bigger horses and started to out grow their two little original ponies.

At some point in time, John had been taught to drive and Joe had learned to pull both a two-wheel cart and a pretty nice one-seated buggy. Along with all of his other chores, he often delivered milk in the town of Twodot. Joe became a delivery horse, getting the mail, bringing groceries home, and often transported the kids to and from school. On a number of occasions, John had given buggy rides to older people visiting in the area who had not had a ride in a horse and buggy since the time that had been their only mode of travel. Upon returning to the area to visit or attend some family gathering, they had requested the pleasure of one last buggy ride through the countryside. John became quite the chauffer and he and Joe had a multitude of their pictures scattered all over the country. Often his trips involved crossing water when creeks and rivers ran high, or when snow banks prevented any other type of travel, but he never failed to finish the trip.

Just about the time Frank and John were expanding their interests to bigger things and other horses, Mike and Cathryn, the two younger kids in the family, were fast developing an interest in Smokey and Joe, and everything for the horses started all over again. Only by this time, they were no longer colts but seasoned and very accomplished kids' horses. Those two kids never missed a day when they weren't pleasure riding, doing errands, and often jobs around the ranch including working horses, sheep, and cattle. It was the absolute highlight in their young lives when they could ride along side either of their big brothers, or quite often with Buster himself, on some ranching chores. It was always pretty easy to make a hand on either of these two little horses as they had been doing this work for years. There's no way to estimate the number of miles those horses put on while working for that family on their own ranch, and worked on all the neighbors' ranches, too. One of the biggest highlights Smokey and Joe experienced was when they worked on the large gathering of community brandings. Each Spring all the ranchers would go from ranch to ranch and help each other with their large herds of cattle; branding, and moving them to the summer pastures. Smokey and Joe took part in them all.

On several occasions, when as kids, John or Mike would drive or ride Joe into Two Dot to get the mail or groceries; they would need to leave him tied for a minute along the main street while they were in the store.

Often times, upon coming back with their purchases, they would run into a man named Austin Pierce who would be standing beside Joe admiring him. Austin was an old ranch hand who had worked for many of the ranchers around Twodot, but, especially, for Twodot Wilson for whom the town was named. Austin had been involved in a train wreck many years before while going east with a load of Wilson's calves. In those days, a cowboy or two went with each rancher's cattle to see that they were fed and watered. The wreck caused Austin to lose his leg. By now, he had grown very old, had tried to run a small harness and leather repair shop, and enjoyed his retirement in Two Dot. He talked with a real serious speech defect; his old eyes had become very faded, though they were still very dark brown. He could look very ferocious to a kid while standing there on his crutches; his little mustache quivering on his lip.

He would say, "I'm glad I caught you boys in town today. Tell your dad that I think this pony is finally fat enough to butcher. I'll be out in the morning to start on him." He really put a scare into those boys as he ran his hands over Joe's hips. Then he'd hobble off down the street on his crutches, probably laughing a little to himself for sounding so mean. It would happen often when any of the kids showed up in town on Joe. What they didn't realize was that he would have easily given his life to defend that little horse from anyone who would even consider doing him any harm.

Year after year ticked away, then a decade, and then another as Frank grew to manhood, got married, and started raising his own family. His endeavors and experience took him into several fields and a number of states, but every once in a while he'd make a stop back to his old country home of Two Dot. By this time he had three small children of his own who, over the years, had grown up to become expert horsemen, but they had all started out by taking their first rides on both Smokey and Joe. The fundamentals and experiences learned prepared them for a lifetime of horsemanship that all three would enjoy.

Cathryn their only daughter also left home and embarked on her career of raising a family of four. Her children also logged their first horseback experiences on Smokey and Joe.

John and Mike both wound up with ranches in the area. Joe was taken to John's ranch where he retired, and lived out the rest of his life running loose on the ranch where he was very much a part of the family. One year, during heavy spring rains, while Joe was running with a herd of other horses, he got bogged down in the heavily saturated ground along the edge of a big reservoir and died. Joe was 28 years old.

Smokey remained on Buster's ranch throughout his life. He watched all of the kids grow up and leave. He saw the passing of many of the family pets; dogs, some of the favorite old milk cows, and horses. He worried some for a while as he saw Joe loaded up and hauled away when he went to live on John's ranch. But Smokey and Buster remained. Eventually, he saw Rose pass away. He learned to know and enjoy the visits of Frank's family and Cathryn's family. Other friends and families who knew John and Frank as kids brought their children over to get to know a horse they had known many years ago. Smokey endured a few more cold snowy winters and hot, mosquito-infested summers. And then one night, Smokey died peacefully in his sleep at 30-years-of-age, right there at home on Buster's ranch.

It took the family a long time before they began to get involved in enough things to put aside and start forgetting Smokey and Joe. It was difficult as they had been there daily to work, to teach, to entertain, and to serve an entire family. They had come down through a little of the history of Twodot country, the Moore family, and the Robertson family who claimed them. They touched the lives of so many families who grew up knowing these two horses. Even the young boys who Buster hired to break and train Smokey and Joe as colts grew to be old men and died in the area. One had become a retired ranch hand and, eventually, a sheepherder. But in telling the stories of their lives, they always mentioned that one of the first horses they helped to break was Smokey and how he had bucked them off. It seems like that is what life is all about; what was, what is now, and what is going to be—the people and things we knew that have come and gone. In a case like this, these horses command a big part of the past. They will never be forgotten.

JOEY HOPKINS

Two Dot, Montana, has only been on the map since about 1900 and, like any typical little ranching town, there have been many individuals, as well as families, that have come and gone over the years. Many of these are incidental and one, in remembering back, easily overlooks the names and faces of those whom were once well-known-perhaps even close friends. As a rule, the old-timers, or the most successful people are the ones you think of right away when reminiscing or telling stories of the past. One person whom I will never forget is little Joey Hopkins.

Joey Hopkins was small for his age and was sickly for most of his young life. By his tenth birthday, he had suffered a kidney operation as well as all the ailments both before and after, which is part of such a sickness. It seemed like he never had much of a chance at life from the day he was born.

His father was a kindly but ineffective man who grew up in the Two Dot area and had already raised a family of four daughters, all of whom had grown up and left home. The parents, Ernest (better known as Slim) and Bessie, eventually got a divorce. Slim, after living alone in Two Dot for a short time, made a trip to California and wound up coming home married to a new bride several years younger than him by the name of Vesta.

The couple lived in Two Dot where Slim operated a gasoline bulk plant, milked a few cows, and had a small herd of sheep. He also used to meet the train every day and carry the mailbags from the depot to the post office, which was located in the town's only remaining store. He was a friend to everyone, and loved nothing better than to stop on the street or gather with others in the store and talk of the old days, or of friends and neighbors who were no longer around.

Slim and Vesta became the proud parents of a daughter, Beverly, and then, about two years later, a son that they named Joey after his grandfather, Joe Hopkins.

For the next 3 or 4 years Slim and Joey were always together. You never saw one without the other. I guess Slim wasn't all that old, he just looked older because he had no teeth, he was pretty fat, and always wore a big pair of bib overalls. He wore an old blue scotch cap both winter and summer and pulled it well down on his head. He peered out from behind wire rim glasses, his cheeks were quite puffy, and his nose was sort of purple, which was due to having spent many years outdoors fighting the elements. But he had definitely found a new meaning in life with the only son he had ever known.

Joey was blond haired and had a little spray of freckles across his nose and talked like an old man. He developed a look as though he had a whole mouth full of some-thing ready to swallow and he spoke very slowly; though his voice was soft, it was deep for a little boy. With his grownup manner and way of speaking, it would always make him seem like an old man more than a little boy of three or four years. But because he was sickly, Joey was always pale.

Slim drove around in a 1936 pickup, which was in excellent condition and always carried a broom sticking up out of one of the stake holes in the box. Whenever the occasion permitted, Slim and Joey would stop off at the local dump and spend hours going through everything that was hauled in there. They'd pick up old motors, clocks, scrap tin, and anything that might be used again wherever it could serve a purpose.

During this process Joey soon began to show promise as a pretty good mechanic. On several occasions he would bring home some old clocks he'd found in the dump, take them all apart, and put them back together again. I guess he had done the same with old washing machine motors and actually get them to running. Slim would smile and his eyes would sparkle as he made it a point to tell everyone about Joey and his mechanical ability. He was very proud of him and rightfully so. Joey never bragged or said much of anything either way. He was very polite and likeable, but he developed an almost apologetic manner for being along with his father all the time.

One year, after Joey had started school, there was a boy, one or two grades ahead of him, who started bullying him and used to give Joey some trouble. But he didn't let it bother him very much. One day some older kids knocked the bully down and, in the wrestling match and scuffle that followed, Joey decided to get in on it. So when the bully was finally held down flat on his back, Joey just slowly walked over and set his foot right down on the ruffian's face. After it was all over and he was turned loose, the bully went bawling to the teacher telling her about the upper grade boys picking on him. This caused a general assembly to be called and the teacher questioned each kid about his part. Finally, after she had questioned everyone and tried to be fair, I think she realized it was just a case of kids straightening out a situation as kids usually do for there was only about five or six boys involved, and they were all pretty good kids. Not one of them was a troublemaker. The teacher then said, "Joey, did you have anything to do with this?" Joey swallowed and very slowly answered, "Well, just that I stepped on his face, but I did it real easy." And that was the absolute truth.

The Hopkins family eventually opened and operated a small filling station about a half-mile north of Two Dot on what was then known as Highway 6. It was one of the main highways across the state of Montana, and I think they did a pretty good business. Vesta and Beverly ran the station while Slim and Joey stayed more or less over at the house and operated it like a small ranch with their sheep and milk cows and a few acres of hay land they had fenced off in parcels around Two Dot.

Slim eventually bought a small International Farmal Cub tractor-not too much bigger than a good-sized garden tractor. He and Joey used it for everything, as it came with several attachments, including a blade on the front and mowing machine. It was very small and weighed maybe about 1000 lbs. But like everything else Slim ever had, he was very proud of it and kept it in immaculate condition. Joey was, by now, about ten-years-old and very capable. He could drive both the pickup and the tractor. He always hurried straight home from school and spent all his spare time working with his father on some project they had started.

It must have been about the summer of 1950. School was out and summer time around the Two Dot area was like any place-busy but a very happy time. Joey and his father were working on a project in their yard at home when they realized the need for a hay wagon that was across the road from the house. As always, Joey so willingly climbed on the little cub tractor and happily started across the yard to get the hay wagon. As he crossed the main street of Two Dot, he had to stop and open a gate to get into the pasture where the wagon was sitting. As usual, there was a slight decline off of the road leading down through the gate and into the pasture. Joey pulled up onto the declining approach, set the brakes on the tractor, and hurried off to open the gate. Just as he was returning to the tractor, he saw it start to move and then began rolling down through the gate toward the pasture.

Joey, small for his age, hadn't been quite strong enough to set the brakes all the way on enough to hold the tractor. By the time he got the gate opened, the brakes gave way and the tractor started rolling toward him.

His first impulse was to run straight up to the tractor and grab the brake pedals with his hands and try to pull them on but the poor little fellow was not strong enough and, in his haste, he ran right up in front of the hind wheel, which caught his foot and turned him face down flat to the ground. The tractor ran right up the middle of him and over his head killing him instantly.

When Joey didn't return with the hay wagon about when he should, Slim became concerned and went in search of his son. He was the first to find him. I believe this to be the worst tragedy in the history of Two Dot. Slim Hopkins could not grasp what he had just found. He broke down completely and never really recovered from the loss of his son. As soon as the word of Joey's death got around, the whole town was in shock. Everyone in the community, feeling deep sorrow for them, came to offer their help to the grief stricken Hopkins family. The little boy whom everyone loved, but just took for granted, had all of a sudden left a vacancy that was felt throughout the entire area, and which hardly anyone could comprehend.

Everyone from the biggest ranches to the retired railroaders begged to do something to try and help ease the pain that this family was now suffering. But there was nothing that could be done. Slim, Vesta, and Beverly eventually accepted their loss and went on with their lives. For the rest of his life, Slim still talked to his son when he was out doing his chores. He passed way a few years later still grieving for his son. I sincerely hope that by this time, Vesta has joined Slim, and they are together again with Joey somewhere in Eternity.

JACK'S LAST FENCE

The old man worked meticulously at this newest project. He was building a long board fence on the north end of his property. He had built many such things throughout his life but this one he wanted to be really right. Old Jack had cut a one-inch square stick exactly 10 feet 6 inches long to measure the exact same distance between each posthole. He had measured the total distance of the fence and divided the area into equal spacing so each span would be identical. Each 6x6 inch post was exactly centered in each posthole and filled with concrete, checked and rechecked for plumb, turned and returned to be standing exactly square with the direction of the fence. He sawed notches into each post lending and aligning the 2x6 inch cross rails and then screwed upright 6 inch picket- type planks to those fittings and again plumbing each one very carefully and accurately. When he was totally satisfied that he had done a flawless job, the fence could only be described as perfect. He painted it a kind of grey color called Sage. That was to him the most perfect part of the whole job. After the last detail was all attended to, he spent the next seven years, every morning as soon as he got up, going out on his back porch looking over his fence and gazing off in the distance like someone searching for something or for someone to show up on a far away hilltop. After each morning's moment, he would turn and, somewhat satisfied, come back into his house and go on with the rest of the new day dawning. Whether in the summer or in the winter, he spent his time staring at his fence just as the dark of night was yielding to the dim daylight and quite often, the end of the day would include seeing the bright red sun just sliding across the full length of his prize fence.

All of his life he had done this same thing—staring at the far away mountains or the trees along the winding river as the sun rose. It had always been his favorite time of day and his favorite thing to do. He said to watch the sun come up on the new day gives you a lot of inspiration, faith and drive. He felt he learned a lot about the earth and what was happening by watching this daily occurrence.

Jack was born in Montana, something he had always felt very lucky about. He grew up there in a ranching family and had learned at a very early age how to work. On any ranch there is always the opportunity and/or the necessity to learn to carpenter, farm, doctor humans as well as animals, and tend to pastures. He learned a little about mechanics although usually left that to someone else more adept at it than him. He had learned to be resourceful at making anything run or limp in the necessary modes to get him home, which almost always meant back to the ranch. He had grown up, both through his own experiences and those of his brothers and neighbors, to be very knowledgeable and adept at just about any task. Of all his efforts and interests, his favorite was handling, judging, doctoring, and, in general, caring for his animals.

Throughout his life this had been his main mission. He broke many horses, bought and sold and raised many herds of cattle; and learned all he could about feeding, breeding new and old blood lines, breeds, and cross breeding. He had in his seventy plus years become looked upon as a pretty reliable authority by those around him.

During those seventy years he had owned ranches, leased some, and quite often ran ranches for others. Eventually, he wound down to just buying cattle, mostly cows and bulls, for all kinds of ranchers. He had worked a lot of the entire west and had connections and clients in many states from Montana to Arizona to Texas and from Nebraska to California. He got to where he looked at it as an attempt at retiring, but actually had built a whole career out of buying and placing cattle and just kind of leaving the actual running of them to younger people.

Another thing that he had watched and learned a lot about but never understood why it was happening, was that ranching and ranches, as he had known it for at least three generations, were disappearing and totally ceasing to exist.

He worried about it every day of his life and could not understand as he watched thousands of acres turned into town sites, parking lots, recreational and wildlife refuges. Ranchers and their families, one after another, sold their old home ranches that had been in their family for generations and had their permits and leases taken from them. As more and more of this happened, he saw big problems over taxes, wildfires, shortages of water, and badly run down pasture land and timberland. He realized that every time one more ranch was eliminated from the community, so were the life keeping jobs of several families. Right along behind that, the loss of more businesses on every main street across the country went out of business, again causing a couple of more jobs for some family to disappear. Then the next thing he noticed was that more homes were up for sale and, more often than not, foreclosed on. It was definitely a perpetual thing that he watched and worried about. He tried to talk to all kinds of people about it but always felt that many of them didn't really notice and most didn't seem very concerned.

Jack was outgoing and pleasant. All kinds of people, not only ranch people, but businessmen, teachers, politicians, and common laborers always lined up to visit with him every place he went. They laughed and listened to his extremely interesting opinions, and recollections and always felt entertained and enlightened afterwards. But when he returned home, or was by himself, he was very worried and felt deep sadness for the turn his way of life that he had known and practiced had taken and changed. He could never really lose that heavy feeling from his mind, but he really didn't change much himself. He remained very optimistic and continually strived to promote and apply the ranching business.

He couldn't stop traveling to big production sales, even to Canada, to purchase high dollar bulls or heifers to be placed on some deserving rancher's program. If need be, he would either lease a place for the rancher that hired him or run the ranch on shares in various parts of the country with very trusted friends from the past as operators. He did the same with horses, particularly good broke working ranch-type geldings. It kept him busy and kept his eyes on the pulse of the whole enterprise concerning ranching.

Jack eventually bought a small place in southern Arizona, which had the real ranch atmosphere but was actually along the edge of a nice quiet little ranching town, where he thought he could just kind of operate there having the best of both worlds. He was out in the hills where people still ranched and yet was close to town and paved streets. He kept his place meticulously neat and had his favorite dog along with several nice horses. He felt very close to nature there.

But after a few years, he realized how fast homes were building up around him, and before he knew it, streets and houses, streetlights, and way too many people were crowding in all around him. He couldn't believe how they built their houses so close together and each family had several dogs, two or more cars, many had a boat, and some had campers. He could often hear bickering and problems between neighbors who didn't even know each other by name. It seemed he had most of their shortcomings and difficulties for his own problems. He had never lived this way and didn't want to do it now. He got word of vandal-izing and thieving and often saw police cars racing into the home sights around him. But most disturbing of all about this busy new way of life was the obstruction of his view of the beautiful landscape that he knew lay out there beyond him. Because of all this, he decided to build his new fence, which would hide it all. Now when he looked out to the north boundary of his own place, his eyes could only see the long neat stretch of fence he had built, just about matching the color of sagebrush. His memory and past experiences reminded him of beautiful grassy hills, winding rivers, or mountain cliffs that he had memorized from his seventy years of ranching in all kinds of country. He could look at his neat fence and visualize any type of setting out beyond it that he wanted to.

Occasionally, he would run into some of the people who lived in the new neighborhood, and while he'd speak some sort of a greeting to them, it never seemed to go over very well. They usually would not return his greeting and would act very unfriendly and suspicious of him. Jack would look at them and feel very strangely towards them and, finally, just turn away and leave them totally alone. He would be upset and wonder where they could possibly be coming from.

On a particular occasion, he was coming home from town one day and noticed a car he knew belonged to one of his closest neighbors. There was steam pouring from under the hood and a large puddle of water under it and realized the car was out of order. He stopped just past it and walked back to the driver's side of the stalled car, preparing to say, "Could I help you or give you a ride?" But he noticed the driver was a middle-aged lady alone in the car. She would not acknowledge him in any way and, in fact, showed much fear of him. He finally just tried to speak through the window to her that he would at least call someone to come and get her if she'd like, but he could get no acknowledgement from her at all. He finally, almost embarrassingly, just got in his pickup and drove on home. He was upset and disappointed that people had actually gotten so distant from each other, that he couldn't even help a neighbor in need whether he knew them or not.

He thought of the number of times when he and his old neighbors might be anywhere from a mile to ten miles apart and would drive through snow banks in the middle of the night to run an errand or help one another. He knew that people needed to be able to count on each other and that it was fulfilling to be there for someone in time of need. He began to feel like he had reached a time and place where he didn't fit in very well anymore.

Jack had an extremely strong urge to talk to people and help or guide them in their daily routines. He wanted to point out shortcomings he could see in their business practices and problems he could see in government and daily living of all kinds of people. He had always felt these things and never passed up an opportunity to listen to speakers, educators, and salesmen. He realized many were wrong and some were quite offensive and pushy. He worked really hard at not being this way and always had his facts and points together and was well prepared. When someone wasn't interested or didn't want to listen to him, he knew it right away and left them alone. He had a long record of people he had coached and lectured who had realized he was well worth listening to. He had spent most all of his life involved with ranch people, and they were always having to deal with state officials, legislators, and, sometimes, just the non-ranching general public. He became the person everyone chose to represent their organizations or cause and tried throughout his life to get him involved in politics, but he never did go that far. At this time in his life he had realized some interest in writing articles for several publications to try to help out certain causes and problems, but decided he'd rather talk to people and represent those that asked for his help. His sole purpose behind it all was that he felt he had something to offer of value, and he'd reached a time in his life when this was the best way for him to be the most help. He was very serious and dedicated to make some mark in time that would be of value to people he knew would appreciate his help.

Once in awhile he would go out and stare at his fence and think about problems and solutions that bothered him. Every so often he thought about the new housing development he had hidden behind his fence, and he felt he'd like to go over and hold a meeting with his neighbors and try to make them see that there was much wrong with their way of life. He felt he knew exactly some of the problems they had; too much money, both Moms and Dads working, and the kids raising themselves with no quality family time such as having meals together or simply doing things as a family. He knew the parents would be gone most of the day and the kids would look forward to them leaving so they could ride around in cars going too fast and too wild. They all had enough money to spend so there was no reason for any of them to think about a job and there wasn't much interest in what might ever be their life's work. If they were home, they just sat and stared at their television sets or were occasionally getting into trouble like robbing some place or maybe getting involved in drugs or alcohol related difficulties.

But he knew that as bad as those families could use someone's help, they would not see any need of his involvement and would look at him as a very unwelcome self-appointed busybody. On a few occasions, he had talked to some of the young kids and almost made pretty good friends with a few of them. He tried hard to give them ideas or steer them into thinking of work or a direction, but then most would go their way and he wouldn't see them again. He truly wanted to make an important difference in their lives, but he knew he wasn't reaching any of them. He could have given them some very good insights into family life, religious attitudes, and a lot of good business and governmental outlooks. He felt very inadequate knowing if he could get just one kid on a better track, it would be worth it. Instead, he felt like he chose to hide behind his big fence and let them drift along learning to fend for themselves.

On one such day, he decided to walk the entire length of his fence and search for some in depth solutions to problems he was dwelling on. As he got down along towards the far end, he came upon a plank that had fallen clear off of his fence and was, in fact, somewhat buried in the sandy dirt and grass. He examined it pretty good and on his return trip back towards the house, he realized there were a few more boards getting pretty loose and one almost cracked clear across. The screws he had used were rusting pretty badly and showing a lot of wear from the weather. He took into account the damage he noticed but kept his mind on the other things he had been stewing over when he'd decided to walk the fence in the first place.

As he neared his house, he heard his phone ringing and hurried on in to answer it. The voice on the other end was that of a woman who said, "Jack, this is Amber Wells. Do you remember me?" He was very surprised as he tried to remember who she might be, and he finally said, "Yes, up there in Trinidad, Colorado." She said, "Yes, I am William's daughter. You remember Dad. I was quite small the last time I saw you." Instantly, his mind took him way back in time to one of his best friends with whom he'd had a lot of very successful dealings and happy memories. The girl's voice went on to explain that her family wanted him to know her father had passed away and they talked on for a few more minutes. After she had hung up the phone, Jack went back outside to sit on his porch and noticed the sun was going down. He thought to himself the sun is setting on another day and one of my dearest old friends has dropped out and has left this life and the plank that had fallen from his fence came to mind. He thought just as my friend has left a vacancy in my life, so has this plank left a vacancy in my most immediate prized possession. His friend had spent more than seventy years living his life doing all that he did, and his fence was probably only about twelve years standing out here, but nonetheless, each served their purpose, and now each was the subject of a big missing link. It was obvious to Jack that day that he would not replace the board and as time went on, there would be more vacancies in the fence.

After a few more months, he could count other old friends who had passed on and just as surely other boards fell from his fence. Some were broken, once in awhile one just broke loose at the top and stood leaning weakly until it finally fell over but still clung at the bottom for a few more weeks before it finally fell out all together. And so it was with men. Eventually, one after another had performed all that was expected of them and they passed away. As Jack sat, or walked out along his fence, he appreciated and admired both his friends and the boards that had fallen.

As he admired his fence and dreamed of a country that he imagined lay way out there behind it, he could also count the boards that were missing and remember friends who thought like him and did things like him and with him, but he knew no longer existed. He still got much pleasure from his memories and fantasizing.

He lived each day and appreciated his own good health and hoped he wasn't becoming weird or insane. But he tried to spend some time each day at the fence and stay strong and active the rest of the time.

Another year passed and one morning as Jack and his dog were walking around his property, he noticed a pickup driving into his yard. It stopped in front of his house and he started toward it to see who had come to visit him. As he walked up to the pickup, three young boys got out looking very serious, but young and strong, also a little nervous as they each greeted Jack and asked if they might talk with him for a few minutes. Of course his reply was, "Certainly." They explained who they were and then told him that they had heard him speak out at times and they had been sent by their high school graduating class to ask him if he would speak at their graduation coming up in just nine months.

Jack was extremely pleased, but asked them a few questions to make certain they really wanted him to do this. He wholeheartedly agreed to do so and thanked them very graciously for asking him. Almost as soon as the three boys drove away, he sat down and began to write some notes. He wanted to prepare the best speech he had ever made and no amount of work would be too much as far as he was concerned. Every few days, and at all kinds of intervals, he made notes, wrote and rewrote ideas and thoughts that came to him as he prepared what he hoped would be the most flawless, motivating, and advising address that he could put together. Soon he began to worry that it might be getting too long. But he was very proud that he had been asked to speak to these young people and though he felt he might not even know many of them, he wanted very much to send a message out to each one of them and hopefully they would remember at least some of what he said for the rest of their lives. He kept writing and preparing, rewriting and rearranging his message until he was sure it was very good and left nothing out that he'd like to be sure they would hear.

He even went to town and bought a new hat and suit of clothes. It seemed to him like this was his one big chance to be heard and to give them a real good set of guidelines and standards to live by for all of their lives. It reminded him of something a father might want to tell his own children if he felt he would never be able to speak to them again. He would have to say everything in this one speech.

The big night finally arrived. Jack drove himself to the high school and was amazed at the number of cars parked out around the perimeter of the school yard. He walked inside and could not believe the size of the crowd. He didn't realize there were that many people in the whole town. He was quickly spotted by some faculty members and was ushered backstage of the huge gymnasium to stand with the graduating class numbering close to two hundred students. He was very proud but kept his composure. Then the ceremony started.

Faculty members spoke, awards were given out, more speakers, and finally the superintendent of schools arose and introduced Jack. He gave a very fitting introduction and Jack arose and walked to the podium.

For an instant he looked out over that sea of people who were prepared to hear his message and he pulled from his jacket pocket the speech he had so faithfully prepared. He noticed that all of the coughing, shuffling, and other sounds stopped and it got very quiet. As he opened his mouth to speak he slid the prepared notes he had spread out on the podium back into his pocket. It was as if he were one of the people sitting in the crowd as he heard his lips say, "A few years ago I built a fence around the front of my property," and then he heard no more as a very warm and interesting message poured from his heart and he talked on among much applause. He would stop for a moment until his audience could hear him again and then he would continue on until another statement would bring about another huge applause. He noticed that when at last he stopped talking, the entire crowd was on their feet and wildly clapping. He finally turned and returned to his seat as many faculty members tried to shake his hand. He tried to leave the school and return to his pickup to go home, but everyone was thanking and congratulating him and he felt he must have done a good job.

He wondered how he could have ever have felt he lived in a time and place when he didn't fit in too well. There was not one person in that crowd of students and parents who could not relate to his message and they wanted to hear more for it was the voice of life coming straight from one who lived it right and to the fullest.

THE STORY OF WILL COOTS

Will Coots was a big man any way you looked at him. He stood six feet four inches and weighed a little over two hundred pounds. But even bigger than that he was looked up to and liked by everyone who knew him. Even total strangers when they first met him took an instant liking to him. Everyone in his hometown saw him as a big, good-natured, agreeable guy who was always willing to be of help. He laughed at life, both the good and bad, and tried to create good will and good feelings among people wherever he went. But biggest of all, he stood the tallest before his wife Jane and their five daughters, who ranged in age from five to thirteen. Dana, the oldest girl, was just going into her freshman year of high school. She beamed with pride each time her father showed up at school to pick her up. All of her friends and classmates would gather around them both to hear Will joke with them. He'd encourage one of the football players by telling him to keep up the good blocking like he did last week against Prineville, or maybe make some plans to take several of the girls along with this own daughter to a swim meet some place the next weekend. She was very proud of her daddy. All of his children depended on their dad for his wise ideas, good guidance, understanding ways, and counted on him as always being there because of his unquestionable love for them and their mother. Together, they made up a very happy household. They lived contentedly in a little town in Connecticut, right close to the New York state line, and knew their neighbors and associates well.

Will had worked at many jobs, from assembly line work to selling insurance, but the Depression had hit and times had really got tough. It was to quite a large extent his good nature and good outlook that were helping him get by when he was offered a job as the caretaker for the large estate of the renowned newsman, Mr. Lowell Thomas. Will was probably the very best candidate for the job, as working with flower gardens and trees in the out of doors was his first love and biggest interest. He did a superb job for Mr. Thomas and had won the news commentator's deepest respect both as an employee and as a man.

Will did his job with great pride and skill and kept the grounds around the Thomas home immaculate as well as efficiently watering each lawn or fruit at precisely the right time. He pruned the trees carefully just at the right time of year, always seeing that each plant or flower had the final touch to improve its chances of bearing the best fruit, blooming the biggest blossom, or branching out to the utmost of its ability. The whole estate always had that sought after appearance like it was an artist's painting taken from the latest home magazine. Will not only fed his family doing this job, but he really enjoyed every minute that he spent keeping the yards and lawns in grand condition.

It was late in the fall of 1931 and he had harvested all the fruits and vegetables from the gardens and orchards;

the lawns were cut and prepared for the on coming of winter. Will had spent every day for many weeks, not even taking off a full Sunday, harvesting the orchards, preparing the trees, getting the sprinklers and hoses drained and stored away for winter. It was important to not only have each item put away where it would be safe and well kept through the winter months, but also so that he would know right where to go for any or all of it next spring the very minute he would be needing it. Will sure loved to do a good job, it was important to him to always do everything the best he knew how.

On this particular Friday afternoon, he was finishing up a few loose ends and whistling a little tune to himself as he thought about the hunting trip he and his very best friend were going to take into the nearby hills. It had been a year since they had last gone, and he and Frank always looked forward to getting out there and enjoying the out of doors. They really didn't care if they ever fired a shot or not. They would pack a lot of good food, take some of their camping gear, which always included their big red wool hunting coats and hiking boots, and just disappear off into the wooded hills where they could be free of the world's problems and pressures. They loved to feel the brisk fresh air of the late November mornings, and enjoyed the fall colors of the trees and hillsides that surrounded them out there that time of year. They could sit around their campfire at night and tell each other of new plans and ideas they had come up with and even some of the good things they remembered from past years. Frank worked across town and didn't get over to the Coots' household as often as either of the men would of liked. Will, being as busy as he always was, didn't get around that much either. So they really looked forward to their hunting trip each fall, even though it would be for just a couple of days. Their families would get together to celebrate the departure of the two hunters, and also their homecoming just in case they should end up bringing back a deer or some game birds of various types. It was a time the families of both men really looked forward to. But mostly Frank and Will appreciated each other's friendship and really looked forward to this event each year.

The big morning finally came, and they loaded down their old pickup with all of the trappings good hunters needed and said goodbye to both families amidst much laughter and joking and drove away from the Coots' household with the intentions of a very enjoyable weekend. They had their plans well made and had gone into a relatively new area from where they had been going for the past couple of years. They decided to set up their camp in a neat little grove of trees where a small spring was trickling from under a large tree root. It was well into the afternoon before they had their camp all set up and had actually gone out into the forest a mile or so from their campsite. They sat down on a stump and talked for a time about the economy of the country, the many starving people they had heard about and seen, all of the world's problems, politics, and about that new fellow, Franklin D. Roosevelt, that the Democrats were talking about maybe being their candidate for the presidency. Will heard many things from Mr. Thomas and was always up on a lot of good news before it was seen in the newspapers or heard over the radio. Will thought maybe this guy would help get the country rolling again. But mostly they talked about their families, and the good things they would do together this winter. They both spoke of their well-being and how grateful they were to be able to say that and also how good it was to be out here hunting.

They both carried shotguns and admired each other's guns and even bagged a couple of birds for their evening meal. They had a very good time and looked forward to an even more enjoyable time around their campfire that evening. Neither had any idea that before this same time tomorrow a terrible tragedy would befall them that would change their entire lives. They finally wandered on back to their camp, and over an open fire cooked the birds they had brought back, talked for a long time, and went to sleep.

They awakened to a frosty, chilly November morning just a little before the sun made any kind of an appearance, built up a nice fire, cooked up bacon and eggs, cleaned up the camp, and went hunting again. They enjoyed the morning, with the sun coming out just warm enough to take the chill away but leaving the unmistakable nip of autumn in the air. At times they spotted a sign of game, either in the form of deer or a few more game birds.

They were creeping up on a covey of birds just ahead of them when the trail narrowed to where they had to sneak along single file for a short distance and down a little decline. Frank had dropped back to let Will be in the lead, hoping his friend might get the first shot at some birds just in case they showed up again before they had the chance to walk side by side once more just beyond the little hill they had started down. He was following right behind Will, looking into the thick brush anticipating that the birds would show up again any second and was hardly aware that he had cocked both barrels on his prize shotgun. Suddenly, a rock turned beneath his foot causing him to pitch forward rather violently. Without realizing what was happening, he heard a mighty roar as his gun had been thrust forward onto a little rocky ledge hard enough to drop both hammers. Both barrels fired at once right into the back of the leg of the greatest friend he had ever had. The violent blast hit Will in the right leg, spun him completely around, and knocked him clear down to the bottom of the hill.

After what seemed like an eternity, Will began to get himself gathered up and realized what had happened. When he tried to look at his leg, he could tell it was very bad and knew he needed help immediately. He looked around to see what had happened to his partner and found himself looking at a man with the most horrified, ghastly look on his face that he had ever seen. In the next instance he saw him tumble forward and roll down the hill landing very near to him. He didn't know if he was hurt or in a dead faint.

Will called to Frank several times and attempted to get to him for a closer examination, but the minute he tried to move at all, he noticed a large flow of blood coming from his wounded leg and pain shot through him like he had never known. He felt sick and very scared and called to Frank again and again.

Finally, he felt his own leg, and began to realize that he was bleeding to death. Desperately, he began to search himself for something to stop the bleeding, not knowing if this would be possible and not really knowing if he had any leg left at all. Will was every bit the big man people had always seen him as. He began to take charge of his hell of a situation. He fumbled for his big red handkerchief, which he always carried, and tried to fashion a tourniquet around his leg. He had never made one and had only heard that such a thing could be used to stop the bleeding. He felt like he was going to faint—he kind of wished that he could; yet he knew if he did, it would be his end. He thought of Jane and the girls and how he wished he was home. How could he ever explain what had happened to Frank's wife, Mary and his children, for he had no idea if Frank was dead or badly wounded? He cursed himself for not being able to crawl over to examine his friend. He decided the bleeding was finally letting up some due to the tight tourniquet he had made from his handkerchief. He turned it even tighter but couldn't really tell how tight it was because by now his whole leg was beginning to go numb. There were many thoughts racing through Will's head. After what seemed like ages passing by but actually was only a few minutes, as he groped and worked on his terribly wounded leg, he began to notice Frank start to jerk and roll around a little. Frank was badly confused and bewildered as he bellowed out in pain and hurt at his friend lying there on the edge of the trail, trying to stop the bleeding in his own leg, which by now Frank realized had been caused by him. As soon as he was able, he went to Will's aid and began to try in whatever way he could to help, but he cried uncontrollably, cursed, and vowed that he could not understand how such a thing could have happened.

Well, it took a while, but the two men together eventually got back to their pickup and Frank rushed Will for all he was worth to the hospital. After a few days of doctoring and many examinations, the doctors made many comments about the condition of the leg and how it was right next to a miracle. By all rights, he should have died out there in that remote area, and it was just beyond belief how he had lived. Yup, there was just no doubt about it; Will had very definitely saved his own life. It was for sure that that leg would not be the death of Will Coots. The doctors and everyone else were truly amazed.

It took many months of doctoring and many specialists examining him, and then finally one day, a very sad old specialist walked into Will's room at the hospital. He very soberly explained to him that the hour of decision had come; they would have to amputate the leg. Everything they could do had been done, and the leg was going the other way. It would have to come off. Will reacted in the same way that he did to everything else in his life. He took it better than any of his family or his friends. Especially Frank.

Frank never got over the terrible shock of what had happened. He felt responsible, guilty, and completely disgusted with himself. He got rid of all his rifles and shotguns. He raised money, selling everything of his own to start paying on the doctor bills. He did everything he could possibly do to raise money. He even tried to find a night job, and did. Frank worked so many hours; he began to have problems with his own family because he was never home and he was beginning to experience a personality change. Although his wife and children were remarkable people, they had problems reaching out to him. Will's family also tried to reach out to the man they knew meant so much to their father. They explained to him that Will had told them many times that what had happened was strictly an accident and nothing more. No one was to blame. Will would go on with his life. They told him many times how badly Will wanted him to come to the hospital and visit him just to talk, work it all out, and forget it. But Frank could not bring himself to look upon his dear friend lying in a hospital bed with his right leg gone because of his negligence. Frank started having nightmares and began to go see his doctor.

He often brought Will's family some firewood throughout the winter. As the months turned into years, Will became released from the care of all his doctors and had got fitted with an artificial leg. He finally went one day to Frank's house to have a meeting with him. He tried as hard as he could to convince Frank that he could never hold this accident against him nor did he want to have it in any way effect their friendship. Though Frank paid most of the hospital bills and for years often did many favors for Will and his family, he could never live down this terrible accident and absolve himself of all the blame.

Will eventually did go right on living the same life and doing the same things he had always done. As soon as he was able, he went right back to his same old job working for Lowell Thomas and did every bit as good a job as he had ever done. The Thomas family had been very concerned when the accident had taken place, and had come to Will's house to assist in any way they could. One of the many kind and helpful deeds they had done for the Coots was to give a large white rabbit to the five girls. It quickly became the family pet, and remained with them throughout the entire growing up of the children as one by one they left home. The rabbit grew older and died of old age in the arms of Mrs. Coots and the youngest daughter some years after the finishing of this story. It's probably safe to say that everyone concerned with this story, including Will, his family, and all of their friends, recovered and readjusted quite well to this hardship; all of them, except Frank.

After a few years Will decided to move to a new location that was just over the New York state line, which wasn't all that far from where they were now living. The Coots family remained very close with all of their friends, including Frank and his family who were by now growing up and moving away from home, and the Lowell Thomas family where he had worked, and had done very well for several years.

Due to the fact that he was so very active and always on the go, his artificial leg began to wear out and was in need of some repairs. Will put it off again for another short time. Finally, a large main pin in the ankle broke, and he didn't have any choice. He would have to go have the repair work done.

So Will decided the best thing to do was to go buy a bus ticket and ride the Greyhound to the city where he had originally been fitted for the leg. He got his ticket and had his plans all laid out to leave early on the 6:45 bus the first thing in the morning. But the night before Wayne and Lillian, who had become very close friends of the Coots, had stopped by for a visit and during the conversation Will happened to mention his planned trip the following morning. It occurred to Wayne that he also had to make that very same trip and why didn't Will just go with him. Then he wouldn't need to find a ride to the repair shop or worry about keeping a bus schedule, and it would be so much better for both of them in the long run. So, Will decided Wayne was right, and he canceled his bus ride. As they made their preparations, they decided to leave a little earlier than the bus would have.

They told their families' good-bye, and Will and his good friend left on a happy trip to carry out their good intentions. It was almost exactly ten years to the day since Will had gone with his friend Frank to their hunting area. It was 1941.

As they hurried through the traffic, which was pretty light that time of the morning, it was still dark as the day was overcast and threatening snow. They talked and laughed at the events of the day, and of the things many people find to amuse themselves when they are with good friends who see each other often and are bound together for a short period of time like on this trip. No doubt, one of the topics, which they may have gotten on, was the fact that it was almost ten years to the day that Will had had the accident causing him to lose his leg, and how he was making the trip today to have the same leg repaired. There may have even been some mention of the fact that he was very lucky to be alive on this day since he had come pretty close to dying on that day so many years ago.

No one ever got to hear about what might have been said or thought, as fate was laid out before them. Not too many miles down the road, while it was still very dark, there was a car with no marker lights or warning device of any sort to let you know that an automobile had become inoperable and left parked on the shoulder of the highway while the driver had gone for help. Wayne and Will were talking as they drove down the road, not expecting any such thing, never even saw the car in their dim headlights, and struck the car straight away. No one knows what may have happened or what was thought or said, but the car in which Wayne and Will were riding instantly burst into flames, and, in no time at all, became an inferno. Neither man could have escaped nor saved himself from this terrible end. It seems that there should be some sort of an omen or sign that this man who suffered such a serious accident and, because of his will to live, saved his own life, would ten years later be killed while attempting to better the same injury that, by all rights, should have got him the first time. Who knows; maybe it was strictly a coincidence. Everyone who knew him agreed that Will Coots had been a real man.

THE OLD TIMER

One thing that hard times often brings about is a kind of bonding between people. Many life long friends and memories have come out of years spent during very hard times, and are then remembered after times got better.

Paul was a man who grew up in both good and bad times. He came from a good old ranch family who had experienced severe droughts, invasion of grass-hoppers, high and low cattle prices, along with raising a family on a Montana Ranch. During this time, they went through The Great Depression of the late 1920s and early '30s. While Paul might have been a little young to really remember it, he sure learned a lot of his ways from people who had survived it and had managed to make ends meet during that time. Anyone who grew up under this shadow of the Depression, darn sure knew how to scratch out a living from his own labors and resources.

Paul did this quite well as he had driven trucks, worked on ranches, did a lot of trading, and any other job he could find to do. He became a very good auctioneer and knew everyone in his home community. It got to be a habit of his to buy a small tract of land, build a house, some corrals, and put a barn or shop on it. His places were always well improved, and he would sell them at a nice profit. He would then look around, find another spot, and do it all over again. He did this a number times and was pretty good at it. As the years slipped by, he realized that he was not getting any younger. He decided to put his hard work toward building a place for himself where he could spend the rest of his days. He also recognized that some people resented the fact he was making quite a bit of money on the parcels of land they had sold to him. They did not realize the expense and the effort that he had put into his finished products. He knew that prices for property were getting higher all the time.

One evening, he got a phone call from an old friend who lived along the Stillwater River about 30 miles from his present home. The old man had simply said that he would like for Paul to stop by and see him the first chance he got. Paul didn't know what was on the old man's mind and wasn't in any hurry to find out, but finally did stop by to see him. They had known each other for as long as Paul could remember. They visited for a little while and then the old man said, "Paul, I hear you are looking for a place to buy." Paul told him that was true, and the old man said he would like to sell him his place. It consisted of 160 acres, a very nice home, and lots of out buildings. The place would put up a lot of hay and had a lot of nice pasture land to go with it. The beautiful Stillwater River bordered the whole ranch; one of Montana's prettiest rivers with fast waters rushing down through it and splashing against large boulders. The whole area was covered with willows and cottonwood trees.

As the old man laid out the details, Paul could hardly

believe his ears. He could think of no place on earth that could fit him any better, or that he would rather have. Then the old man told Paul what his price would be, and that really stumped Paul—the price was thousands of dollars below the market value! Paul questioned the old man about how he had arrived at his asking price, and the old man answered, "This is my price, this is what I am asking, and I want you to buy this place. Do you want it or not?" Paul ended up telling him he would for sure take the place, and they shook hands on it. Paul left to go home and get his money together. He could hardly contain himself or believe what had just happened. He was extremely happy, but puzzled by his old friend.

In a day or two, he got a phone call from the old man's son. He ranted and raved at Paul on the phone and accused him of trying to steal his father's ranch. He ordered Paul to stay away from the old man, as it was obvious that he was no longer of sound mind. In fact, he said, if anyone was going to buy the ranch, it would be him and not some land grabber or opportunist the likes of Paul. Paul hung up and decided that he would go see the old man about this latest development. As Paul explained to his old friend about his son's call, the old man just shook his head and said, "If I had wanted to sell this place to him, I would have done it years ago. I want someone to have this place that will take care of it, and who is not a drunk. I want to sell to you, Paul. We made a deal and shook hands on it. Now you go home, put your money together, and don't pay any more attention to my son or anyone else."

In a few days, the deal on the ranch was done. Paul and his old friend were signing their names on all the papers. They shook hands once more and headed out the door of the attorney's office, both happy with the deal they had just made. The old man stopped in front of his pickup, asked if Paul had another minute, as he would like to tell him a little story. Paul was interested in hearing the old man's story, so he climbed into the pickup.

"Many years ago, maybe about the time you were born, we were experiencing what is now known as The Great Depression. Your Dad and I were neighbors and very good friends. I'm telling you, Paul, not one thing was worth anything, and nobody had a dime. There were no jobs, and many people were starving. There were thousands of people standing in soup lines all across the country. Your Dad and I helped each other put up our hay and bring in our crops. We never could decide why we harvested the hay we had grown, because sheep and cattle were worth about half of what it cost us to put it up. There was virtually no market for grain or for animals that would use the feed. The entire country was broke. We each survived with our families because we raised whatever we ate. One year, your Dad and I threshed a small patch of grain I had grown. He had a magnificent big black team of horses. They were a lot bigger than my team. Just as we finished threshing, it started storming, and it looked like winter was setting in.

"I asked your Dad what he was going to do all winter, and he said he did not have much to do. So I showed him a piece of land I had over North of where you live now. It was covered with tree stumps and brush, but if cleared off, could make a nice meadow. I told him if he would clear it this winter, I would feed his team, and pay him when things turned around, and maybe we could make a few dollars. He agreed and pulled out all the stumps, burned the brush, and covered up all the holes. We farmed it, and in the spring, it turned into the fabulous hay meadow you see today. But the country was quite awhile getting straightened out, and when things did improve, we had a lot of debts to pay. Your Dad passed away before I could get him paid for what he did, and I have lived a long time since.

"I know my time is probably not too far off, and I didn't know how I would ever square up with him. I don't know what lays ahead for us, and I don't have any idea if your Dad will ever know; but this little land deal of ours is a way that I can help to clear away this debt between me and him. It's the best way

I can see to do it. He can't receive the money, but you are his son, and it will help you. Now you know how I arrived at the price, and I feel very good about it, as I hope you do. Well, Paul, let's go home as we both got moving to do."

Paul is still at home on the land and enjoying it daily. His old friend has joined his father and they are together again in eternity. Hopefully, they are both at peace and not having to fight another Depression.

FRANK'S
BIG DECISION

veryday a person hears a story or a situation that inspires him to comment on, kind of expound with an opinion whether or not he can speak with any kind of authority. As someone wanting to write something of interest to readers, I heard about a challenge that a big name promoter in the horse world threw out there and my mind went immediately to someone very close to me. In answer to his challenge, I want to tell this true story, as I remember it, about a man and his horse that lived and accomplished things way beyond myself. I hope the recipients in this story will in some way appreciate my good intentions.

The man's name is Frank, and he has been through more than 70 winters. He never spent any idle time but was able to carve out a life through scruples, hard work, figuring, and scheming, even when hardships prevailed or things didn't work out as planned. But his successes far out numbered his failures and he continued to forge on daily.

One afternoon while visiting with some friends, one of then told Frank of a meeting he had attended involving some powerful promoters of the American Quarter Horse Association. A question one of them wanted to throw out to the public and have people call in or write about was this, "If you could take a ride on any horse that ever lived, which one would you like to ride?" When the conversation occurred between Frank and his friends, it didn't make much of an impact, and in a few minutes Frank went on about his day's work, eventually coming back to his house. It was getting on into the evening, so he fixed a little supper, sat back to catch the evening news, and relax for a few minutes before bedtime. Tomorrow would start early again and end up being a long, hard day.

As he started to enjoy his well-earned moment of relaxation, the question kind of came back around in his mind, and he gave it more thought. At first very little and then quite a bit more as horses like Secretariat and other big names in cutting, reining, racing, and war horses from throughout history began drifting through his mind.

No doubt the same way big names of horses got to circulating in his memory, so did memories of past experiences; his eyes immediately went to a large painting hanging on his living room wall. It was a picture of a big sorrel gelding eating an apple out of the hand of a young cowboy. The painting was the work of a very close friend of his who also happened to be quite a famous artist. She had known both the horse and the cowboy in the picture very well and had certainly recreated on that canvas both of the subjects exactly as they had appeared in real life at that time so many years ago.

Gradually the evening news got blotted out and time started turning back in his mind and soon it was early spring in a very familiar area of Montana along in the late 1950s. A baby colt was born on a familiar old ranch located in very good country. Under Frank's old gray hair and through his eyes, the past became very real once again. He saw the start of early green grass showing through what was left of last winter's snow banks, magpies flying and flitting about keeping close track of the new foal and his mother. The day offered the first warm sun and the promise of spring yet still turning pretty cold at sundown and on into darkness. The colt was healthy and grew fast. Summer finally arrived with lots of mesquite, some rain, and good green grass. Frank saw himself in his dream riding the new colt's full sister, whom he was just breaking. He often saw himself talking to the old rancher, Buster, who owned the mare and the baby colt, and also to Jack Smart who owned the stallion, a Dan Patch bred horse. Frank, himself, was probably in his early 30s. He was at the time managing and operating a pretty good-sized feedlot in a place called Shepherd, Montana. He rode daily for long hours doctoring, sorting, and shipping his pens of several thousand head of cattle.

A few years sped through his memory and he remembered how the little mare had gotten into some moldy silage one night and he had found her dead the next morning in her pen. Old Buster had told him to come by and get the big sorrel gelding as a replacement. He'd have to break him, but he had grown up now to a 2-year-old and was ready to make a horse.

Frank got him and named him Kickapoo, possibly after a famous bucking horse by that same name, but the name stuck and usually the horse was just called Kick, for short. Thus started a career that lasted more than 30 years and thousands of miles for Frank and the big gelding.

In no time at all he was working cattle, opening gates, had a rope swung on him, wore out his first set of shoes, and started developing the look of a veteran ranch horse. There was no job he wouldn't do or hadn't done; he knew his business and just kept getting better. He grew tall and rangy, probably reaching 16 hands, and weighed more than 1200 pounds. He had a nice stripe on his face and had tall white socks. He was every bit as pretty as he was good. Frank had proudly branded him with the R Bar on the right shoulder, the brand he had inherited from his grandfather of the same name.

Frank by now had a wife and a nice family and owned several head of other horses. Some he mounted his kids on, some he just rode a while and then sold, and others he kept around to use himself, but old Kick was fast becoming his top horse.

Eventually, the feedlot started to play out and while Frank had many friends, ranchers, and traders in the area, he had become to all of them their right hand man. He gathered many cattle for a lot of them, often riding a pretty good portion of the Crow Indian Reservation land, which a lot of these ranches and friends leased. He rode up and down the Yellowstone River and a lot of the country in the Pompey's Pillar area which was famous from the days of Lewis and Clark. Old Kick was his top horse in all of this and at times Frank even played a little Cowboy Polo.

Then one day he loaded up all of his family and belongings and moved to Nebraska. He took a job there on a large ranch and feedlot, again involving many long days in the saddle. At one point, in heavy rainy weather, he rode all night keeping the big fat steers in the feedlot from bogging down in the mud. Because of their size and weight, he had to keep them on their feet. He often told how he'd have to rope them to pull them back onto their feet if they laid down for too long, being so heavy they couldn't get back up on their own.

The ranch and feedlot called for a lot of horse back riding and cow work and lasted a pretty good while. Frank and Kick moved on to Los Animas, Colorado, where they ran a large ranch running about 500 Hereford cows and a large bunch of Mexican steers. This ranch, too, required a lot of long days in the saddle for him and his horses. He met people here who were influential to him and his family for the rest of his life.

He met and became well-acquainted with Hank Wiesecamp, promoter of the famed cutting horses, Poco Bueno and Skipper W. Frank knew these people and horses personally, and survived the same experiences right along side of him. Kick knew all of Frank's good and tough times, especially when his wife left him and moved to California with their children. But Kick stayed behind and saw all the kids come back to visit and, eventually, remain again as a family. There were some really good friends involved and at times Kick might move in and stay with some of Frank's rancher friends for a week or two or maybe even a month. But eventually Frank and Kick found themselves enroute to Rifle, Colorado, for a spell at dude ranching and then on to Wheatland, Wyoming, to run a very large historical outfit which had been a big part of the old Swan Cattle Co. of Nebraska and Wyoming history. Together they experienced the problem of working a large ranch where the owners had no knowledge of what they were doing or what ranching was all about. Together they endured the same frustrations and disappointments.

They wound up spending a few years in business for themselves and finally set out for Canada, a very big move and very far away. It doesn't take long to recall a number of years out of a man and his horse's lifetime and can't even comprehend the amount of miles and experiences they had lived through over the past 10 years of their lives. Frank and his boys, when they could spare a rare but pleasant vacation, took Kick and a couple of their other horses into the Bly Horn Mountains around Story, Wyoming, for a fabulous camping and fishing trip, which was one of the most pleasant memories everyone involved could ever remember. Then to suffer a very bad accident on the way home when the trailer the horses were in was hit by another motorist, all of the horses survived it okay.

In all of these years and miles there were often offers from a lot of people who would have paid a lot of money for Kickapoo, but Frank always turned them all down as he and Kick grew closer—that event became something that would just never happen.

After their arrival in Canada, a whole new life started for the two of them. Frank became the owner of his own ranch and leased a lot of country. He ran cows and calves, yearlings, raised a few horses, and became a very successful veterinarian. He also did a lot of other outside jobs, some involving Kick and some not. But Kick, in his own existence, learned to live with muskeg, bears, moose, and listened many nights to the howls of wolves. He experienced the Northern Lights as well as long winter months, short daylight hours, and deep snow without the winds to bare off the ridges. Kick also endured the extreme north's cold temperatures and grew heavy long winter coats of hair to compensate for it. Years went by and, eventually, it was another 10 and then 10 more. Kick began to realize and experience some rheumatism as did Frank. During this time, Frank had seen to it that Kick had a barn to stay in and plenty of warm blankets, but the years were telling on them both. They still rode and worked together but there were also other horses for some of the longer and harder jobs.

There came a day when old Kick began to wander

away from his warm barn and out into the vast country-side. He seemed to forget where he was or lose his way back home and Frank felt maybe the old horse was disoriented at times. He would bring him home and then have to go hunt him up again the next evening. He even forgot to come in to water. His teeth seemed to have given out and his condition suffered.

Frank began to argue with himself about the job he realized was becoming more necessary, but he was dreading the thought. He knew that Kick was in need of his help as he was reaching the point of suffering. He had hoped Kick would make it through the winter into one more spring and some good green grass but that can take a lot of time in the severe winters of the North Country. Frank finally realized that the fateful day had come. He followed old Kick out to a magnificently beautiful park surrounded by great huge trees and, after setting with him a long spell, he gave his old friend a shot of some stuff he knew would send him into a deep and painless sleep, but a permanent one and he did it. He sat alone and watched the best horse he had ever owned head on out over the great divide into his eternal place. Kick had been with him for 34 years.

Frank began to stir and, having fallen asleep in his favorite chair, wiggled and squirmed a little to get the pains and kinks from his own rheumatism out of his joints and got out of his chair. As he started off to his bed, still half asleep and half awake, he passed the painting on his wall and, with his dream so fresh in his mind, he realized what horse he would give anything to be able to take one more ride on above any others that had ever lived and, with that thought deep in his mind, he fell into his bed and went to sleep.

Looking at one more day just past and another big day in the morning.

RUTH AND HER REASON TO GET UP IN THE MORNING

Ruth had got up a little earlier that morning for no real reason, although a little earlier meant 9:00 AM. She had made a cup of coffee and started her usual sitting on the couch and watching to see what her neighbors were doing. She hadn't even gotten around to turning on her TV yet. But she had gone into her usual feeling sorry for herself pretty heavy, which of course was getting her no place.

She had no idea on earth that this day was going to be the beginning of a complete change in the rest of her life. Ironically, all of her everyday habits and routines were going through her mind like a last time occurrence because it was getting ready to be a very hard time with uninvited changes. She was on her way to a badly needed uplifting.

Ruth could actually sit for hours and not be able to think of one thing in her life that she could be happy about. She wasn't very pretty. She was at least 60 lbs. over weight. She had an unhappy childhood, no friends, had never in her life held a job, and didn't even like her name. She once said she saw a TV story where a strange and crude man rode an old mule he called Ruth and that's where she thought her name came from. She felt that her mother had named her that out of spite. She lit a cigarette, which she smoked many of daily, and she had a way of hanging it from her face looking more repulsive and slovenly than anyone could have ever have practiced or rehearsed. She felt that the world in general owed her that.

Ruth had been born to a lady very much like herself. She couldn't remember ever having seen her father, but had heard many stories from her mother about how useless and worthless he had been. She grew up assuming she had no reason to ever want to know him. She had lived with her mother until she was about 18 years old and really didn't even have much use for her. They fought a lot, and she could remember having to continually listen to complaints of how miserable and mistreated she had always been, and the fact that she was very sickly. Her mother had always depended on some type of city, county, or state subsistence money to survive. There had never been enough to provide for any type of frivolities and she knew better than to ever ask for any. Before long they started fighting because her mother insisted that Ruth help around the house, doing dishes and cleaning to earn her keep. But Ruth developed an attitude that her mother was supposed to be raising her and why should she be waiting on her mother. She had quit school and had been expelled a time or two by the sixth grade. Once, when her mother realized that Ruth had stolen a pack of cigarettes, she kicked her out into the street all together. That was just the beginning of the end of their living together. Ruth wound up with her own welfare checks from then on until her mother passed away. She became another ward of the taxpayers from the age of 18 years until the present time. She hated the thought that she was now 43 years old. She, just like her mother, was not at all healthy. She suffered from backaches, stomach aches, depression,. and her eyes bothered her. She felt sure that she also suffered from migraines and high blood pressure. Sometimes she wondered if she didn't have diabetes or possibly some fatal illness lurking around in her body that would one day strike her dead. On occasion doctors or the county nurse diagnosed her as being healthy except for inactivity and obesity. She quickly told them that they were just not very thorough. Of course, she argued with them when they told her to quit smoking and to get some exercise. She was not a happy person and did not like herself.

She was sure that the welfare people resented her for the money she received and that they felt they were a lot better than her. Her answer was to tell them all to go to hell.

This morning Ruth was just turning on the TV when the loud knock on the door startled her. She immediately figured it was her neighbors as she had called the police on them last night because their dog had been barking. She figured that it wasn't right that someone's dog could bark and keep her awake at night. She just knew that they would really be mad at her and she prepared herself for a fight. She pulled her heavy housecoat around her and stomped to the door and prepared for the worst. But there at the door stood a small well-dressed man. With his hat in his hand he quietly asked, "Ruth?" She stepped outside her door and pulling it shut she defensively answered, "Yes?" He said, "Ruth, I am with the state department and

I need to visit with you a minute. Would you mind if I came inside, as I have a few things to talk to you about." Instantly, Ruth became suspicious. The last time someone like this came to her door it had been the landlord. He had asked to get inside and got her evicted when he realized that she was not taking care of the house. The words "State Department" set off an alarm in her mind. Her policy had become to not talk to them at all.

She said as rudely and officiously as she knew how, "We can talk just fine right here," and then added, "because I haven't got anything to say to you anyway." The man, who said his name was James, just smiled at her and said, "Our governor has adopted a new program for people receiving substance checks, and, under the new law, anyone receiving any monies will report for work and will be paid according to the job they do. From now on there will be no more free money handed out. You will still receive your income, but you will be assigned a job and starting this Monday morning, will earn every dime you receive." Ruth frowned and fussed, "I am not even well enough to work. I have no skills or education, and no way to get any place to work. I hardly think that's going to apply in my case."

She was just starting to explain to him how the government people always resented her receiving the check, and how someone always had to butt into her affairs. James just skillfully out maneuvered her and said, "Ma'am, those are exactly the things that we are out to fix. We have so many people and so many jobs out there that you could qualify for, but first we will enter you into a training program that will fit all of your abilities and short comings." He was totally polite with her and had an answer for every one of her excuses. He never raised his voice or demanded anything of her. Out of lack of anything else to say, she eked out the question, "What kind of job?" He said, "Ma'am, anything from fighting fires to babysitting little children. We will give you some tests and place you wherever you will fit the best." After a little more explaining and detail, James promised her he would be back to pick up her at 8:00 AM next Monday morning and that no excuse would help. She would need to be dressed and ready to go. Ruth was speechless and scared almost beyond words, but she had nothing else to say. James smiled and put on his hat and politely said, "Good-bye Ruth. We'll see you Monday morning." After he left, she let herself back inside and began to worry. She tried to think of every alibi and excuse there was to get her out of the Monday morning appointment. Before she knew it, Monday morning had arrived. At five minutes to 8:00, just as James had promised, a lady driver appeared at her door and told Ruth she must come with her. Nothing made any difference. Her dress, whether she felt good or not, whether or not she had any money, nothing. She received a check from the state to live on and was now in line to start performing a service for the privilege. Reluctantly, Ruth got in the van and went with the other people they had gathered up. They were all taken down town to a type of classroom. There they were interviewed, tested, and doctors and councilors checked some of them. It was a very thorough and efficient screening process. After a few days of this for Ruth, she had an appointment with a very nice young doctor who checked her over for all of the ailments that she could describe to him. At last he said to her, "Ruth, I am very sure we have gotten to the root of your biggest problem, and I have some medicine here that I would like to try on you. Take this for three days and come back here to me on Friday and we'll see if they are helping." She did just that. On her appointed day, she was back in his office and had to admit that she had indeed realized much relief from at least some of her pains. She found the doctor to be quite pleasant and believed that she had finally found one that knew something. He gave her a new five-day supply of the pills and had much advice and comforting talk for her. She was kept very busy with the screening and interviewing. Everyone was so considerate of her fears and self-consciousness that she felt rather pleasant about most things that they were telling her. She began to look at the whole situation much differently than she had expected that she would. She found that all of the people who talked to her were truly interested in her welfare.

On the next visit to her new doctor she admitted to him that her back had not bothered her, she had no more headaches, and she thought that she generally felt better all around. He sat her down, took her hand, and explained to her that he wished he could give everyone of his patients the diagnoses he was giving her. He said, "Ruth, you are very healthy; you have only imaginary ailments which come from lack of activity. The pills you have been taking are only sugar pills and have no medicine in them at all. That is the best news you will ever hear coming from your doctor." He gave her a pep talk and the name of a good counselor. At first, she was embarrassed and mad. But he told her that psychological ailments were quite common and needed to be treated. He could easily understand how she felt. He was happy for her that her health was good; he did not degrade her or put her down. When she left his office she had already begun to consider losing weight, quitting smoking, and exercising. For the first time in 43 years Ruth had a lesson in her own self-preservation and image. She was beginning to see the world in a new light.

The next morning when she came to her new surroundings, she was ushered into a room with three other people whom she had started with. A large, but very firm, fair lady in her late 50s took them to a desk and sat them all down. She called each of them by their first names and then said; "All of you people show great potential in filing, research, and office management. So, we are taking you over to the Veterans Hospital where you will be in charge of records. It will be your job to locate old and lost records and to organize and categorize new ones." She then explained to them the importance of accurate medical records for the benefit of the veterans and their families. Lack of these records is depriving thousands of our veterans of the medical treatments and recognition they deserve. It will be your job to fix this problem. Much of what she was saying went right over Ruth's head because of her lack of experience, but to her surprise, she detected within herself an interest. It occurred to her that maybe she could learn about this important sounding mission. For the first time in her whole life she felt a little twinge of excitement.

They took her to her office and started her out. She nearly had to relearn to read and write, but they started to teach her a few basics on the computer and, to her surprise, she learned fast. She really applied herself to her newfound interest. One of the most important things she realized was that she really liked this new boss lady whose name was Dorothy. Ruth learned from her and listened intently to everything Dorothy said. She began to realize personal habits and practices from her as well as how to do her job. She soon began to look forward to coming into work in the morning. Just as Dorothy had told her from the beginning, each day patients would come seeking her, some of them crippled and ill, most of them older veterans who had no records of who they were or if, in fact, they were even veterans at all. At times some of them passed away before the doctors could see them.

Ruth learned of avenues to seek out their histories and developed ways to get them enrolled in the hospital and started on their care. Soon she felt that she needed to be at that hospital earlier than her appointed hour and she willingly stayed later than was expected of her. All of this because she knew that it was important to someone in need. It was not long before her supervisors, patients, and even she herself could hardly believe the things she was getting accomplished. Everyone was amazed at her new attitude and interest in her new work.

Ruth took on a whole new look. The prettier she became on the inside made the outside improve twice as much. She firmed up in muscle tone and lost many pounds. She learned to apply makeup and got a new hair do. And most of the time she wore a smile. She acquired some new clothes, with the help of Dorothy and the others, and began to dress very nice. She often times had long and interesting conversations with her co- workers and patients, and at times she even joked and cut-up some. Ruth was on her way and coming into her own. After she had worked about two months, Dorothy caught her as she arrived at work a half hour early. "Ruth!" Dorothy exclaimed. "You and I have a meeting this morning at 10:00 AM. It is very important and involves some good new for you." She took Ruth by the hand and said, "I am so proud of you." Ruth could hardly wait to see what Dorothy was talking about.

At 10:00 o'clock she went to the conference room. Dorothy was already there with the administrator who Ruth knew only by sight. She joined them and there was an air of much happiness and excitement. The administrator gave Ruth a lot of praise and told her that she had been hired by the hospital. He said, "Ruth, the job you are doing is excellent and we want to put you on salary, which will be more than twice the subsistence you are currently receiving. And you will receive all of our benefits, including insurance, retirement, and vacation. You are no longer on any kind of welfare. You will be subject to a quarterly raise over the next year and a half if you decide to stay with us, which we hope you will. Again, for the tenth time in the last several months, Ruth was speechless, but grateful. At that moment, no one would have recognized her as the same lady whom James had spoken with outside her home that morning a few months ago. She had really changed and all for the better. She continued to progress and had many experiences, both with happy and some not so happy endings.

Then one morning an old man was brought to her desk. His name was Vince and, although he was obviously very sick, he was an interesting and likable old man. He simply told her that he felt like he had become sick enough to come to the hospital, but did not tell her much else. After some coaxing and questioning of him, she learned he was a World War II veteran and in his early seventies. He had not been to a doctor since he was wounded and released at the close of WWII. Ruth liked this man instantly and wanted to get him some help. She had the feeling that he could really be interesting if she ever got him started telling his story. She started searching for any information that she could get on him and got him enrolled with a good doctor. But there seemed to be no sign of any records on him. She searched for days and weeks without any kind of success. She questioned him some more and about all she could get from him was that he had fought the Japs and spent his time on all of the islands. Nothing she could ask him about seemed to get him talking. He never mentioned anything that he had ever done or seen. Ruth exhausted every possibility that she knew of to try to obtain some proof of his past military existence and was always met with the same answers; no records, no such person, and no past history,

Vince was getting worse, although he was receiving treatment, it did not look good. She had spent enough time with him that they had become good friends. They both realized their strong relationship. He had thanked her many times for all her efforts and usually ended up saying, "You know, Ruth, I doubt that it's worth all this trouble. I am sure that even if they kicked me out of here today, the results would be about the same. I believe whether I'm lying in here or in some cheap hotel room, I'm about finished. I appreciate all you have done." He never once complained like others had. Even though he had given his years, effort, and some of his good health for his country, no one cared. In fact, when Vince opened his mouth to speak, he only had positive things to say. He once spoke of his wife and son, who were now both dead, and that he was all alone.

When Ruth returned to her desk, she recalled a resource she had once used in a similar situation. It was a line that would take her to a place in Washington DC called the archives. In her mind she pictured a huge basement with large stacks of boxes each filled with lost service records. She knew you had to be extremely lucky to get any answers back from them at all. But she remembered the success she had with them before. Once again she gathered her information on Vince and called them. She was told not to sit by the phone but they would see what they could do. She answered, "You damn well know that I'll sit by the phone until I get the information that I need." And she did.

Each day Vince lost a little more ground and each day Washington told her they couldn't find anything on him. She responded each time with, "Well, go take another look."

A little later in the day she was having a problem with a man who was cussing and condemning her. He felt the hospital was inadequate, the doctors didn't are about him, and he doubted if she had tried at all to arrange for his records. Then her phone rang. "Hello, this is Ruth," she waited for a response, but was met with silence. Then a voice from Washington said "Bingo! We made a find on that fellow Vince that you have been calling us about. We not only found his paperwork, but he is in line to receive a Distinguished Service Cross for his efforts in saving a company of men and a pilot that was shot down on some little unknown island over in the Pacific back in 1944. We are sending out the packet to you immediately." Ruth was so excited and happy that she smiled and laughed with the complainer sitting at her desk. Finally getting him pacified and on his way, she raced straight to Vince's bedside. She told him of the good news and mentioned that he had won a medal.

He stared off into space and didn't say much. "I forget about those, Ruth, I have a couple of them already." Then he gave her a little speech about the things that he did over there that were heroic. "By God, Ruth, all I ever did was what had to be done. I sure didn't do anything that any of the other guys wouldn't have done. All any of us did was try to survive. None of us were looking for any medals for killing people." Then he stopped talking; Ruth really admired him. She knew that he was sick, but yet he was very strong. When Vince's packet arrived Ruth had all of his records and his medal. The hospital had a cel-ebration and presented him with his belated medal. He accepted it very graciously and seemed quite pleased. For a few days Vince kind of improved. He and Ruth visited and she learned a lot from him. Then one morning, though it was not her place to do it, Ruth decided to stop in his room and see how his night had been. She quietly stepped through his door and noticed he was sleeping. She tipped toed over to his bedside and, upon closer examination, she noticed that he looked very peaceful. His right hand was lying across his chest clutching his newest medal. He had passed away in his sleep. For a very brief but seemingly long moment in her life Ruth closed her eyes and realized a scene or scenario, which she had never seen. This man she was gazing down upon had exercised quite a lot of out of the ordinary effort in doing what was expected of him by saving the lives of several of his fellow soldiers and comrades and that according to the records, he had done the same thing on other occasions. He did it all for no other reason than to be doing the best he could and what he knew was the right thing to do. Any medals or recognition which came from his acts had no bearing at all and he shunned and put down the credits others had given him.

For the first time in Ruth's life she felt a large measure of satisfaction in herself for having applied extra effort and going beyond normal everyday expectations in having found these records and making for Vince his last hours just a little more memorable and enjoyable. She felt a sort of rush for having done the best she could and having applied herself more than normally. And she felt she had learned a huge lesson; that good things come from going the extra mile.

She felt rewarded and grateful that she had accomplished so much, though hardly anyone would ever realize or benefit by her actions. But she now had a whole new attitude about accomplishing things. She knew she would savor that attitude for the rest of her life. And she had learned it all from a very accomplished man who came along very late in her life and was now already gone forever-except in her memory and list of experiences. While she felt no credit was due, she felt highly rewarded. A feeling she was definitely not used to.

She looked at this man laying very still and wished that she could have met him a long time ago. She wiped some tears from her eyes and pressed the button for the nurse. As soon as the nurse arrived, she would head on down to her office to start another day. She knew there would be more people in need of her help. She felt glad that she could be there for them. It felt good to be busy and she realized that a person needs a reason to get up in the morning.

On her way down the hall to her office, she ran across a little orderly named Johnny whom she knew quite well. Stopping, she said, "Johnny, do you think you could go with me on Saturday for a couple of hours?" To which he replied, "You bet I could, Ruth! Where are we going?" "I'm going to go downtown and buy my first new car."

AFTERWORD

"THE LITTLE CRIPPLED MARE"
by Mike Robertson

The old man sat down on a little grassy
    plot,
Spread out all around him were grandkids
    he loved a lot.

They asked him, "Tell us, Grandpa, the tale
you tell with care,

It is our favorite story, the one about the
little crippled mare."

The man turned his weathered face up to
search the skies,

And drifted to another world as he slowly
closed his eyes.

The man started speaking, and said, "It
greatly pains me,

The things I try to describe, I know you'll
never see."

A world of cows and horses, rivers, trees,
snow and rain.

A world of great people, much love, good
times, and a little pain.

In 80 years I've known a lot of good horses
all along the way

But the very best was the mother of a little
one we just called the little bay.

She was a sweet soul we called the little
crippled mare

And she raised four colts, each one special
and rare.

Shortly after the little bay was weaned
however, she had to be put down

Immediately we knew that the thing to do
was to always keep him around.

A boy in a wheelchair came to live on the
ranch and the little horse knew when
they met

AFTERWORD

He had a big job to do and his work was not
finished yet.
She had taught him well, that little crippled
mare,
How some folks in life needed a little extra
care
The boy grew and got healthy, with the
help of the little bay,
Spending time outdoors, in the sun, almost
every single day
The boy and the horse were an inseparable
pair,
Eventually it happened that the boy no
longer needed his chair.
The old man had tears dripping on his face
As he told his grandkids of that time and
place
And about how the little bay horse taught
the boy how to care
All stemming from the love of that crippled
little mare.

CPSIA information can be obtained
at www.ICGtesting.com
Printed in the USA
FSOW01n0927131214
3865FS

9 781627 870573